StoryBoard

The Restoration Of Jonah

Kevin Hansen

kevin.storyboardproductions@gmail.com

Design by Kevin Hansen

Edited by C Brooke Brassell

To my children,

Mallory, Schyler, Holland and Brooklynne.

You have always been my inspiration.

Preface

I suppose there are times in all of our lives that a moment of inspiration comes to us in a variety of ways. The idea for this story goes back over thirty years, when I was a young boy with a love for history. I remember wanting so badly to someday be able to find a treasure, and what that might entail. But growing up in rural Idaho, buried treasures were few and far between, so my attention changed slightly to sports. Well into my married life, I went back to my love of history, and I began researching various topics. One day, my treasure map finally arrived. It was the story of a treasure, the person who buried it, the people over time who searched for it, and then, finally, the people who discovered it.

It is a story about not only finding a treasure, but also finding the treasure that is buried deep within all of us: oneself.

I would like to thank all of those who inspired me in various ways with this book. Some of that inspiration came from the experiences of my past, some came from encouragement in the present, and some was drawn from things yet to come.

But especially for M, thank you for everything.

The Restoration of Jonah is the story of a man who, while in search of something hidden somewhere in England, along the way tries to find himself again, after years of being lost.

The Prologue

I stood in the doorway, almost as if expecting someone to say something before I left. The wooden planked floor creaked as I slowly shifted my weight from one foot to the other, and then I paused. The silence in the room only mirrored her response. She never came, she didn't call out to me, and she never would again. Not that I could blame her.

Monica hadn't been back to my apartment in over two weeks. I missed her, but deep down I knew begging for her to come back would only delay the inevitable.

I had met Monica three months before, after standing in line at El Pollo Guapo, one of those make-it-in-front-of-you burrito places. I noticed her immediately. She stood in line ahead of me, absorbed in her phone. She was in her late twenties, around 5 feet 7 inches, with beautiful blonde hair that fell over her shoulders. Eating seemed to be a distraction to her. She only looked up to order, then she became merged with her phone again.

I sat facing her, a couple tables away, mesmerized by her beauty, but almost as much by her intensity. She almost ate without taking her eyes off of whatever was drawing her to her phone. After a couple of bites, I noticed a smear of avocado had remained above her upper lip. I cleared my throat, getting her attention, and then gestured to her with a napkin and by wiping off my own lip. She stopped chewing for a moment, finally recognizing the reason for my movement. She moved her napkin to her mouth, wiping away the smeared guacamole, and as her eyes widened she looked back toward me and mouthed, "Thank you." I smiled and went back to my own burrito, trying not to stare, glancing up occasionally to find her back to her phone. It wasn't in my personality to approach women, but especially women I didn't know. I sat wondering how to approach her. Then she suddenly stood.

She's leaving, I thought. *Another missed chance.*

Then, to my surprise she walked past me, sliding her business card under my hand. *Monica Paulson Home Designs.* I stared at the card, then looked up at her as she walked out the door, pausing briefly to look back at me and smile. Her hair blew in her face as the door opened, and then she was gone. The card remained fixed in my hand, and then I turned it over and read:

"I would love to hear from you."

It was fast and furious in the beginning, with Monica and I seemingly not being able to get enough of each other. She had finally been able to slow down a bit from the helter-skelter lifestyle she had created for herself since college, and I had opened up a bit after three years of first and second dates since my twelve-year marriage had collapsed. We spent time going to art galleries, going out to dinner, and dancing, and we even had taken a couple of long weekends just to get away, anywhere, as long as we were together.

Then it happened, again, like a virus waiting patiently inside the body, waiting for the most inopportune time to show itself. I slowed down the calling and the texting. Work in my studio required more of my time. We only went out a couple of times a week, and then this relationship virus attacked completely.

I would now go days without calling. Monica's texts would go unanswered, and then she stopped. She stopped trying. This vicious cycle I was in sounded a lot like a record with a scratch, repeating parts of "Lost in Love" by Air Supply over and over and over. But I did it; I slowly pushed away the best thing that had been in my life. And now she was gone forever.

As I began pulling the door closed, my eyes scanned the apartment, looking to see if there was anything that I had forgotten. My eyes stopped when I spotted the lone airline ticket sitting on the breakfast bar. My heart sank. I stared at the ticket momentarily, and then slowly began to shut the door. The morning sun lit up the entire apartment, contrasting with the darkness of the hall in which I stood. As I slowly pulled the handle to the door, the floor beneath me moaned as if my soul had begun to mourn, and slowly the stream of light coming from my apartment became darker and darker, symbolically extinguishing any light left in my relationship with Monica. The door finally closed, and with one last tug clicked shut, seeming to echo down the silent hallway. My heart, quiet for two weeks, went silent.

Why am I doing this? I thought.

I picked up my computer bag, throwing it over my shoulders and resting it on my back, pulled up on my suitcase, and began the quiet walk down the hall to the staircase and the four flights of stairs down from my apartment. The light of the day and warmth of the summer sun in Boston shook away the effects of the emotional morning, and my taxi arrived at the curb, perfectly on time.

Chapter 1

The "ding" sound of the" fasten your seatbelt warning" is what awakened me. I slowly peeled my eyes open, noticing that the British Airways flight 5982 was finally over land again. I hadn't been able to sleep much once the flight left Boston, but somewhere out over the Atlantic Ocean I had fallen asleep. A copy of Fodor's Historic England rested open, spine-up, against my thigh, and my body felt like it hadn't moved for hours.

I looked over at Mrs. Collie, a seventy-something Mrs. Doubtfire-looking grandmother on her way home after visiting family in Connecticut. She smiled back. "Did you have a pleasant sleep?" she asked.

"I did. Thank you," I replied.

Mrs. Collie had spent most of the early flight telling me about visiting her daughter Louise, and Louise's husband Eric, who had attended Cambridge and graduated in something called nanobiotechnology. They had married shortly after graduation, moved back to Eric's native New England to work, and now Mrs. Collie traveled over at least once a year to visit her growing grandchildren.

I sat quietly listening to story after story about Mrs. Collie's homeland of England, her husband, and the two hundred year old home that they had bought back in 1961, or was it 1962? She told me of growing up in Hungerford, Berkshire, west of London, where

I should go, what I should see, and a nice neighbor lady, Juliette, whose husband had died of cancer over a year ago. She was sure that Juliette and I would "get along splendidly!" I broke into a little smile, just listening.

Her stories and voice reminded me of a female narrator, had *Winnie the Pooh* been narrated by a woman. It was a nice escape for me, finally being able to relax and take my mind off of the empty apartment that I had left behind, and the same one that would be waiting for me on my return. I suppose that the calmness of her voice eventually lulled me into a haze, and Mrs. Collie took notice and I eventually drifted off asleep somewhere over the waters of the North Atlantic.

My eyes opened, focusing out the aircraft window, fixed upon a land below; a foreign land, but one that I felt like I knew almost like the back of my own hand. I loved England, and had from the time I was a kid. I loved the stories of my own grandmother moving from Liverpool, crossing the Atlantic aboard the U.S.S. Cretic, and then settling in a town north of Boston near Maine.

Shortly after my divorce, I went back to school and finished my degree in medieval studies even though my photography business was doing extremely well, but there was something missing. So the idea came from Monica to go to England. She had noticed the hole in my life that she, at times, felt swallowed her as well. Two weeks of driving, two weeks of exploring, and two weeks for us to try to fill that hole together. But two weeks before the trip, the sinkhole grew, almost swallowing everything in its path. The relationship was unable to get out of the way.

The flight began its rainy approach to Heathrow International and I was still unsure of what direction to go once on the ground. All that I knew at this point was that there was a single ticket sitting on my table at home, and an empty seat next to me, one that should have been Monica's.

The cabin came to life as if it were the village of Brigadoon, finally awakening from a dreamy coma. The plane rested in place. Passengers stood stretching, tugging at the knees of their pants, pulling out the bunched up fabric from their hips, and children were jumping in place trying to get the blood pumping back through their bones after the long flight.

I remained seated, knowing that I had nothing but time, no plans, no one expecting me for dinner—or breakfast, for that matter. The anxious crowd of passengers filled in the center aisle, moving slowly as one large mass like a herd of cattle. Finally, I picked up my carry-on, pulled it over my head and shoulder and waited for the last of the crowd to move ahead.

Chapter 2

I was thirty-six when I found out. Twelve years of marriage seemed to crumble all in one night. Day by day, week by week, and month by month, the blocks of my marriage to Diane seemed to be as solid as any couple might want. There were PTA meetings, Little League seasons, homework assignments, family camping vacations—everything that any other "normal" family might experience. We had two great kids, Lilly and Dawson.

It was a day in mid-April, 2009, when I found a greeting card tucked away in the nightstand on Diane's side of the bed, underneath a stack of Yoga Journal magazines. Nothing too unusual for Diane to have a card; she was given them all the time. Diane worked as a fitness instructor, teaching Pilates, yoga, and an occasional spin class, but the cards mostly came from her Senior Fitness class. They were cards of thanks, cards of encouragement, but mostly cards given "just because." But this card felt out of place—hidden, but almost out in the open at the same time.

I picked it up, sliding the magazines on top of it off to the floor. My hands shook, almost knowing of its contents. My eyes scanned the front of the card, then opened it to see the writing enclosed. A scene from Mutual of Omaha's Wild Kingdom is the closest thing to compare to that experience, with Marlon Perkins being consumed by some anaconda in a South American river, struggling to breathe, being suffocated as the creature wraps itself around him over and over, then beginning to squeeze.

Gasping to breathe, feeling my heart pumping harder and harder to supply the needed oxygen to my brain, I collapsed sitting on the bed. Three months later, it was over. I had decided to stop, stop trying to make someone else love me, stop wondering where Diane was at every minute of the day, stop trying to figure out why she loved another man instead of me, and stop crying every day. I wasn't sure if it was because I was tired of it, or if there just weren't any tears left to cry.

Chapter 3

As I walked slowly toward the luggage area, I must have looked a lot like Augustus Gloop eying the river of chocolate: completely mesmerized. The signs, the shops, the female voice over the airport audio system—all were postcard images that I could have filled my studio with. There was the elderly gentleman wearing a tweed jacket and tie with a matching kilt, and the group of twenty-something year old friends sporting their neon green Mohawks and skin-tight black pants, reminding me of a music video from The Cure.

But the sounds were what really entranced me. Most people try to avoid the sounds of crowds, the unnecessary chatter of thousands of people, cars honking, airplanes taking off and landing, but I began swimming in it. I listened to the children crying out loud to each other with their innocent Cockney accents, the restaurateurs calling out order after order, and the casual conversations of individuals everywhere, sounding as if they spoke the original language of the angels. I wanted to just stop, sit down, close my eyes and take it all in. Just like Augustus Gloop, I wanted to swim in this river of audio chocolate. I could just spend two weeks, just here, listening and watching.

The rain slowly let up as my Jetta pulled out from the Hertz lot onto the A2. I had been in many places alone, for extended periods of time, but fourteen days of being alone in a foreign country by myself was quite a bit more intimidating. Images of Monica sitting in the passenger seat flashed through my mind. This was supposed to be "our" trip. Just the two of us escaping from the schedule, from constant phone calls, but more than anything, it was supposed to be our chance to see what life was to be like together all of the time.

A BMW honked, quickly bringing my focus back to my American driving style, merging into an oncoming British car filled road. Turning corners seemed to be the hardest part of driving in England. All of my attention was needed to focus on the road in front of me. No more drifting off into a life behind me or even a life waiting for me in the future. It was all about the here and now.

My/our travel plans originally had called for most of the sightseeing to take place outside of London. It had been my desire to explore castles, the countryside, the quaint postcard bed-and-breakfasts, and the emerald green countrysides divided like a puzzle by centuries-old stone fences. I didn't want to get lost in the mass of people in the surroundings of London. If there was time for that at the end of the trip, that would work. The places I wanted to go were the places of the stories from my childhood. They were the stories told to me by my grandmother and my grandfather, who came from a small fishing village of Somerset County, located on the northern coast of the Cornish peninsula, and the small villages of Berkshire County. London on this trip was an afterthought.

Chapter 4

1066 AD

The year was 1066 A.D. The northwest coast of France lay silent, with the only interruption being the hypnotic sound of the waves keeping time along the beaches of Normandy. Torches were lit every hundred yards, producing an eerie glow that stretched for miles, illuminating the fog that had set in overnight. The mid-September setting couldn't have been more ideal, William thought. With his army of eight thousand deeply asleep, William paced slowly, peered out the door of his tent, and went over in his mind his plan.

~

Once a week this was her job. It was about her favorite time of her week. Herleva was twenty three, and the oldest of three children. A basket sat next to the shore of the Ante River as she pounded the wet clothes against the smooth river rocks alongside the bank, cleaning them. The river was peaceful, slowly moving away from her. It mirrored her life, she thought—slowly moving, not knowing from where it came, or where it was going. Herleva's eyes rose up, gazing across the river, watching as a handful of geese flying up river flew close to the water. The green valley across the river, along with the sounds of the slow moving water, put her soul to rest each time she came to wash. The unique sound of the wind moving through the tree-lined river provided a daily melody each time to her ears, with today's being a soft lullaby as a faint breeze brushed against her face.

The river, or at least the escape from her other chores, was a much-appreciated break. The feudal life of peasants was nothing more than the life of slaves without the physical chains. Mondays Herleva and her two younger brothers and parents spent in the fields of their local monastery, plowing the fields, planting the crops, and harvesting. Her youngest brother Pierre's job was to walk through the fields wearing a wooden yoke with buckets hanging from both ends, collecting unwanted rocks. This is where it started, the life of one destined to live and die chained to the land with nothing but a short leash of freedom. Pierre struggled, as he barely stood tall enough to make the wooden buckets clear off the ground. Soon enough he would learn, as they all did, to collect equal weight in each container so that the yoke would not spill with its own imbalance. Jacques helped his father with the donkey and plow, learning to guide, steer, and work the land as their father did as a child, and his father, and his father, and so on. Herleva and her mother worked in the kitchen making breads and stews for the monks. In the heat of the summer the kitchen became its own oven, with the stone walls insulating the room from the inside and out. Herleva would stand over the dough to make the bread for the week, with perspiration slowly gathering momentum as it left her brow, trickling down her nose, she quickly caught it before it fell with a quick turn of her head to the sleeve of her blouse.

This scene was reenacted on Tuesdays and Wednesdays, with the family providing feudal service to their lord's lands. So when Thursday, Friday, and Saturday arrived, Herleva's family could focus on plowing their own fields, harvesting their own crops, clearing their own rocks, and baking their own sub-nutritious breads. Their life was one of cooking with inferior grains and eating the leftovers of life. That is what they were, the leftovers, the peasants born into a system of no progression, living in the same place, working fingers, arms, and legs to the bone, generation after generation. Herleva's father was one of the lucky ones; he had managed to outlive death at birth or in early childhood, and at thirty-eight already surpassed the average lifespan of a normal peasant in medieval Western Europe of twenty-eight. Through *the wear of this peasant existence, it seemed as though each year lived equaled three years of distress on the body.*

It was vacation for Herleva as she arrived at the river. This was her break from the dirt of the fields, the sweat of the kitchen, and the noises of her younger brothers. It was a time that her mother had cherished years before, but when she saw in her only daughter a small light of curiosity she passed on to Herleva the joyful task of doing the family laundry weekly. Her father complained about sending their oldest, most capable working child out to wash, but her mother had insisted.

The heat of the mid-September sun bore down on Herleva, and the river called out to her. Her feet were the first to answer, feeling the slick river rocks underneath as she walked cautiously further into the river. The water slowly moved up her legs as she picked up her long flowing skirt from mid-thigh, trying not to get it wet. A movement from the plant growth near the shore startled her, a duck and his mate taking flight almost directly toward Herleva. She stepped and turned quickly to get out of the way, catching her toe under a sharp rock, causing her to lose her balance and land on her side in the cold river. As she stood near the basket, she began taking off the layers of her dress and the tattered undergarments that her mother once wore.

With her clothing drying in the reeds, Herleva moved her body out slowly toward the deeper area of the small cove where she did the wash. The cool water felt refreshing running against her mature body. She lowered herself beneath the surface, moving out into deeper waters, becoming Aegir the water goddess of the ancient Norse mariners. This is when she felt the most freedom, moving beneath the surface floating freely. She stood up, feeling the sand beneath her toes and steadying herself against the current. She looked longingly across the river to the green valley wondering what was out past the horizon. A horse neighed behind her, startling Herleva. Quickly she lowered her body back into the water, turning her head to see near the shoreline a horse with a dark figure sitting on top. The sun reflected off of the water into her eyes, making it nearly impossible to see.

"Have you finished your duties?" the dark figure asked.

"Yes, I have," she answered, with the slight sound of chattering teeth.

"Come here, then," he replied.

Herleva slowly moved toward the river's edge, using her hands and arms to cover up as much of her nakedness as she could. She walked directly into his open arms and he wrapped her gently up in her now dried clothing.

Robert, the Duke of Normandy, held her tightly, running his hands down Herleva's dark brown hair, which matched his own. Robert was the lord to her family—her lord. Like Herleva's, Robert's life was also one of generational repetitiveness, only it was one of wealth and power. While her father looked old and tired, Robert reflected youth and rest. Her father was frail and thin, while Robert was healthy and well-fed.

Without a word said, Herleva backed away from Robert and walked toward a spot where her clothes had been drying amongst the reeds. She sensed the power that she held over the Duke as he began following her almost under a spell. Herleva picked up her clothing as she moved through the reeds. Robert watched as her body moved through the waist-high growth, her back lean and toned from hours and days of work. She turned to look at him, her hair pulled down from her normal sash flowing over her bare shoulders. She smiled and sunk down out of view. This was Robert's cue. As he moved effortlessly through the reeds he found Herleva lying among the spear-like growth on her back. Robert knelt down, joining her.

Herleva quickly dressed, and Robert made his way back to his horse, retrieving a sack hung on the side of it. She carried the basket filled with the freshly washed clothing and met him near his horse. His arms grabbed her, consuming her once more before he left. "The events of today finished, tomorrow brings our future," he said as he set the sack retrieved from his horse on the top of the basket.

The sun was setting as Herleva walked into their single-room, dirt-floored hut. Her father and mother looked at her with an air of question and concern. The sack was emptied onto the eating table, revealing ham, dried fish and real bread, a feast for this family of peasants. "Get ready for dinner, and put your clothes on the table," her mother told the family. Her parents didn't say another word, and neither did Herleva. The food was rationed, with some saved for the days ahead, and then the family went to bed, laying in straw, all five in the family on the same floor, as well as six chickens and a cow.

~

The sun broke through the cracks of the sod walls, warming Herleva's face. Her father had been up for hours milking the cow and starting with the work for his day. Her mother came close with a damp cloth to wash her face. Herleva smiled, looking down at the infant wrapped next to her that she had given birth to only hours before. Her brothers gathered around her, mesmerized by the baby boy that had magically come into their lives.

Hoofs pounded outside. This was not the sound of her father hooking up the donkey. Sabine peered through the crack between the door to the hut and the wall, and her face went white. All she could say was "Herleva." The door opened slowly and Robert walked in, with his dark beard hiding his expression. He walked slowly toward the mother and child, kneeling down and taking the infant into his arms. Quietly he whispered, "Guilliume." The nursemaid that had followed Robert into the hut stood next to him, and he handed her the swaddled boy.

Robert touched the face of Herleva, holding it tenderly, then stood quickly and shouted to his companions on their horses. They dismounted, bringing with them sacks of meat, cheeses, breads, and a small bag of seed: wheat.

As the Duke rode off with his entourage, Herleva's mother stood in the doorway watching the dust raise up from the hoofs of the horses. She turned back to her daughter, moving quickly and holding her gently. Herleva's father stopped long enough to rest against his plow as they disappeared, and then his eyes moved toward the hut.

Herleva, exhausted, rested quietly, only whispering one word as a single tear moved down her face. "William."

The sun was not quite up, and the army was ready. The ships had been stocked the day before and the alarm sounded to prepare to launch. Eight thousand men moved forward toward the ocean. The Duke stood tall on a platform, admiring his huge organized army in front of him. In a whispered breath for only himself to hear, he said, "The events of today finished, tomorrow brings our future." And with that, William, the Duke of Normandy, son of Robert and Herleva, launched his army from France toward the southern coast of England, and toward Hastings.

Chapter 5

The doors on the wooden clock opened, with four two-inch tall royal guards, or Beefeaters, as they are commonly called, emerging with their red coats, miniature rifles over their shoulders, and tall black fur hats, marching out from the bottom compartment of the antique timepiece. Each high-marching step signaled the clock to strike another chime, causing me to stir. The tiny guards, after four chimes, turned and hid themselves again, waiting another hour to be called back on duty.

My body hadn't adjusted to the time difference when I peeled my eyes open slightly to survey the new surroundings. The smell was the first thing that caught my attention. It was the smell of mothballs, a smell that reminded me of long weekend visits to my grandmother's house as a kid. My grandmother, having immigrated to the United States as a child from England, was the only person I knew of that used mothballs. *Maybe they are a British thing*, I thought.

I had arrived late in the evening at Pevensey, situated on the southern English coast, sixty miles from London. During our preparation for the trip, Monica had found an online service that allowed customers to pre-purchase nights through a bed-and-breakfast company that had hundreds of locations on their network. It was to give our travel the flexibility that I had wanted, not knowing how long we would want or need to stay at any location. All that was required was a call in advance of your arrival to verify if a room was available. I had used the B&B guidebook as soon as I landed in London to find a location as close to Pevensey as possible.

I found Battle Bed and Breakfast after calling two others with no rooms available. Battle Bed and Breakfast, I thought, wasn't exactly the most romantic sounding place, but it was perfectly situated in an ideal location for my first day of exploration.

I stretched like an awakened cat, my arms stretching above my head and my toes pointing straight down off the edge of the brass four-poster bed. My 6-feet-4-inch frame wasn't really made for a twin-size bed. I had been told the night before at check-in that the shower was down the hall to the right...or was it to the left? I couldn't remember. My memory either was frozen from the long Atlantic flight, or from the mental arm wrestling I had done with myself as I had driven while trying to stay to the left side of the British roads when my brain and instincts wanted so badly to go right. It had taken its toll.

Only two of the four rooms were occupied before I arrived, with one of the rooms being occupied by a couple from Louisville, Kentucky, here celebrating their honeymoon. Ginny, one of the house owners, assured me that they were at the far end of the house and wouldn't be a bother. She winked.

The room was simply decorated, with a dark-stained dresser, a single wooden chair with a fabric-stuffed seat, and black-and-white photos of the house throughout the years, along with other photos of Pevensey. I walked around the room trying to wake up and found a guest book that sat on the dresser with entries of previous visitors.

As I flipped through the pages, I imagined them as floating ghosts still here in the room as I read through some of their names.

James Upton, Virginia Beach, Virginia, November 1, 1982; Doris Buckhead, Dublin, Ireland, May 29, 1994; Boris and Natasha Ovetchkin, Belarus, March 30, 2009. I added my name to the growing list: Jonah Marks, July 30, 2012, Boston, Massachusetts, USA. I walked to my suitcase, pulled out a pair of green Boston Celtics sweat bottoms and a plain white V-neck t-shirt and put them on so that I could go take a shower. I had brought my own towel, not knowing what each house would provide, picked it up with my bag of toiletries and quietly opened the door to the hallway.

"Lord Jonah! Good morning," came the call of a cheerful voice of an unknown man that had originated from down the hall. My toes dug into the tan shag carpet, frozen as if I had been caught in the kitchen sneaking a cookie from my grandmother's cookie jar, with the slightest sound bringing her attention to my theft of one of her famous peanut butter chocolate chip cookies. My toes released their grip on the carpet, and I walked in the direction of the voice.

"Good morning?" I responded with a slight hint of question. The dark hallway was lined with framed photos, family crests, and cheap prints depicting fox hunts from the 1800s. If I didn't know any better, I would have sworn I was standing in a home undergoing one of those estate sales that I had been to that came with a free self-guided house tour. I expected over-priced tags on each item on the wall of mismatched artwork. The aroma of coffee and some kind of pork product frying grew stronger as I peeked my head around the corner.

"Sorry, lad. I am so used to the creaks and noises of this house. It becomes a habit to say something. Harold Coalchester," he said, introducing himself as he extended his hand after wiping it off on the apron he was wearing. Harold was a tall, slender man in his seventies, with a friendly voice and an even friendlier face. He reminded me of the actor who owned the pig in the movie *Babe*.

"No worries, it just caught me off guard for a bit. Living alone creates a certain solitary life that you get used to," I said shaking his hand.

"Breakfast will be ready shortly. We are serving muffins, poached eggs, bacon, and strawberry preserves," Harold announced.

"Sounds delicious. I haven't eaten a full meal in almost twenty-four hours," I said as my eyes moved around the small kitchen. It was small, at least by my standards. Antiqued ivory cabinets were divided by a newer faux stone countertop, and I noticed the various appliances and their variety of colors and makers. The unique wall decorations seemed to be making more sense.

"So you met Ginny last night?" Harold asked.

"Yes, yes I did. This is quite the place you have here. Have you been here long?" I asked.

"No, no, no. We bought this place after I retired. Ginny has always wanted to be south, closer to the coast and London, and closer to the grandkids." Harold pointed to pictures of his three grandchildren attached to the refrigerator door by three Liverpool Football Club magnets.

"So, you're not from around here?" I asked.

"No, sir. Born and raised up near Warwick," Harold answered as he cracked the brown eggs into the poacher. Harold looked comfortable in the kitchen as he moved preparing breakfast, wearing a pair of casual khaki slacks, blue and pink stripped polo shirt, and a white apron that had been loosely tied with the strings hanging down in the back to his knees. Harold continued. "We retired three years ago and bought this place. I was in education. I worked for forty years, retiring from the Elon School for Boys as the headmaster. It's just right outside of Liverpool. This is close enough to London, but far enough away, if you know what I mean."

I shook my head in agreement, thinking back to the traffic that seemed to flow out of London the night before like thick, slow-moving blood being pumped out from a heart, thinning out slowly the further you moved away from it.

"By the way, the strawberry preserves are straight out of Mrs. C's garden," he proudly announced.

"Awesome. I'm sure they are delicious," I responded.

"So what brings you to Essex?" Harold asked.

"History…Lots of history," I answered.

"Well, you're certain to find it around here," replied Harold.

I looked down at my feet, realizing that I had no socks on and was standing on a cool floor; goose bumps began multiplying on my arms.

"You know, you can't turn around here without bumping into something historical," Harold laughed.

I smiled back. "Anything that I should keep in mind?"

"Well, of course there is Battle Mount, the site of our country giving way to the Vikings via Frenchmen." I noticed a hint of sarcasm in Harold's voice.

A rustle of newspaper came from a small room that was adjacent to the kitchen, and my eyes moved to see a woman sitting and reading, with only the top of her head extending above the top of the newspaper.

"Oh, I'm sorry. I haven't introduced the two of you. Jonah, this is Gabriela, our other guest." Harold walked toward the archway leading into the sitting room that Gabriela occupied. Harold motioned with his hand for me to come closer.

"Jonah?" Gabriela asked.

"Yes," I answered.

Then in that instant I froze again. Not from the cold moving up my legs from the cool floor, but by my sudden realization of my current disheveled condition. My hair was a mess, and I stood in the archway with a towel and toiletry bag, and Gabriela was beautiful. No, actually, she was gorgeous. I made a few futile attempts to pat down my messy dark brown hair to no avail, and then Gabriela smiled at me in my current state of discomfort.

"Buongiorno, Jonah," she said.

I was almost speechless. Gabriela stood about 5 feet 8 inches tall, and I would imagine she was about one hundred and thirty pounds. Her dark brown chocolate hair flowed down to the small of her back, her skin was a golden Mediterranean brown, and she smelled of olive oil. I wondered if Gabriela used olive oil as a tanning lotion.

"Good morning, Gabriela," I replied.

"Oh bother!" Harold belted out. "My eggs!" He quickly moved around me back into the kitchen.

"So what brings you to Battle?" I asked.

Gabriela began to reply, and I found it difficult to concentrate. The black fitted pullover and black Capri pants clung to Gabriela's body like the eyes of every man that looked at her, I thought.

"I am here doing some research," she answered.

"Can I ask you about what?" I replied.

"Well, I am an educator. I call myself an architecurologist." Gabriela laughed. I loved it. I hadn't really experienced a laugh for a number of weeks. "I watch the progress of modern digs of buildings from the Roman Empire and put presentations together to give teachers the most updated information available."

"Is there some kind of dig going on around here now?" I asked.

"No, when it is slow, like it is right now, I go to unique locations and do some additional research for a book that I am putting together."

I admired the way that Gabriela spoke. She was a woman who I could tell had been viewed as nothing more than a beautiful woman for most of her life. She was at the point of just speaking through those men that she spoke to, eliminating the come-on's and ogles.

"So where are you visiting?" I asked.

"A local bathhouse from the first century. And some other small sites," she answered.

"Interesting," I added.

"What about you? On vacation?" she asked.

"I am doing a bit of research myself," I answered.

"For a book?" she asked.

"No, I am actually a photographer. Here to shoot some pictures and put some pieces in my mind together. I've studied so much about this place. I just wanted to see it for myself and put some things into context. Pictures from a book can only do so much. You know?"

I could feel the coolness of my feet change to warmth. The small sitting room Gabriela had occupied was actually a sunroom, with big windows making up most of the wall space and extending to cover half of the ceiling above. The sun had warmed up the tiled floor, and I could see why this room had attracted Gabriela.

"I wish my family understood me like that. They don't understand me and my love for putting the pieces of things together." Gabriela spoke of how she went to school initially to become an architect, and then took a class on Roman architecture that focused on the Age of Empire and the structures located outside of the Italian Peninsula. She had fallen in love with history at that point through structures.

Mr. Coalchester walked back into the archway, hearing the end of Gabriela's thoughts. "I love history! But most of all the history of the greatest ensemble of musicians ever put together—The Beatles!"

"I thought you would say that," I answered.

"I went to primary school with George," Mr. C. added.

The three of us sat and ate the breakfast prepared by Mr. C. Mrs. C was out running errands, and I never thought again about my dark brown messy hair. I excused myself from the table and jumped into the shower, but the images of Gabriela remained in my mind. Once dressed, I went out to say goodbye, but Gabriela was gone, and once again I hadn't asked her anything more about herself. And I wished that I had.

The smell of the salty ocean breeze filled my nose as I opened the car door in the parking lot at Battle Mount. It was a beautiful summer day, and I was comfortable in a pair of jeans and black V-neck t-shirt. I threw my camera bag over my shoulder and started the trail to Battle Mount.

Chapter 6

1066 AD

The winds finally blew. The port of St. Valery, France, had been bursting at the seams, almost as if the Norman will of William alone exploded toward England across Oceanus Britannicus, drawing with it the winds that would push William's army across the English Channel.

William shouted, "With God, all things are possible."

The previous summer months had been spent in preparation for this day. William had collected a hungry but superstitious army from all corners of Europe, and they had waited on the coast of France for the order to sail toward England and collect what William believed and knew waited for him there—the crown of England.

Now, finally the winds were in their favor, pushing them rapidly toward a land that William had dreamed about and that was now within his grasp.

William's army came to shore on the southeastern coast of England, at a place that was renamed Battle. Maybe the name should have been Short Battle, or Not Much of a Battle, but that would have been too strange, although there is a place along the Orkney Islands to the north that is called Tongue of Gangsta. But I digress.

King Harold II of England had heard that William, the Duke of Normandy, was heading toward England to the south. With his worn out army having just fought off and defeated a Norwegian army to the north, Harold marched his tired group of wounded soldiers toward another army two hundred forty-one miles to the south, only this was a well-rested group of soldiers and mercenaries that lay in waiting.

They sat on opposing hills with a green valley separating them, England's past looking straight across at England's future. William, with his well-trained archers, eventually took control, with Harold and his army pushed up their hilltop as the arrows rained down from the sky like the drops of an everyday rainstorm along the same coast.

Legend has it that Harold was shot through the eye and died there on that grassy hill, and soon the rest of the English army surrendered as well.

Now, William the Conqueror was justified. His victory had taken less than a day, which meant that God himself had wanted this victory over England, and now God was using William to further his own desires in this place.

"We must find that which we came to possess," William said, speaking to one of his favorite generals.

"My lord, we shall look under every rock and bush until we have it for you," came the reply of Robert de Beaumont.

"Very well. With God, all things are possible," William responded.

Chapter 7

Two things stood out to me as I approached the Battle Mount Memorial: the overwhelming green growth, and the enormity of the place. Two opposing forces had been here a thousand years before on two opposing hills. One English army, weary from previous battles, almost perched on their hill like a treed bear climbing higher and higher with each bark of the hounds, and the other, a Norman army on the offensive, a rested, well-trained army, hungry for victory, barking louder and louder.

England's King Harold's hill came into view, and I could see the remains of the wall that had surrounded the altar that William had erected in memory of the newly fallen King. The mounds stood about two hundred yards apart and reminded me of the skill of these ancient archers. Thinking back to my class at Boston University, I remembered the details of the English and their archers. As part of their national defenses, it had been mandatory of all men in England to practice archery at a distance of two hundred-fifty yards. In fact, golf, in its infancy, had been banned by King James I because the sport had taken away from archery practice. Those archery practices had come to England with William and the Normans from France.

The early morning moisture of the grassy fields had long since been burned off by the warming sun, and I walked from one ridge to the other slowly, imagining the short but fierce battle that had taken place in this location. Few visitors had arrived in the morning as I walked, and I wondered if it was because of the fact that it was mid-week, or maybe because the site was becoming a piece of forgotten history. This large grassy area in any other location would be a large park, with picnics, the tossing of flying discs, and dogs on a leash being walked by their owners. Trees lined the bowl created by the two opposing grassy ridges.

The heat of the summer sun and my steep climb up to the top of the mount created beads of perspiration, and I was sure that I was in better shape than this. I attributed it to the heat of the sun, something that I wasn't planning on experiencing in England.

The stones that made up this altar seemed out of place for this location. As far as I could see it was nothing but green foliage—grass and trees—and the rocks were rough and jagged, glued together with an ancient mortar that had been repaired a few times. I sat down, resting my back against the memorial's wall, placed in the exact location as legend has it that King Harold of England had fallen dead with an arrow through his eye during the battle with William's forces. I wondered how this scenario felt to a native Englander, as a foreign army had invaded their native soil only to be beat them down after a single day. Your King is killed and you are now under the control of a new regime. That was something that I, as an American, had never had to experience.

The sun bore down on me and the rocks, and heated the wall up to a point that I could feel the heat pressing through my shirt. I started to stand, bracing my hands on the bottom of the altar wall. Suddenly, I fell back toward the jagged rocks with my hands sliding off their hold, and the back of my head slammed into the wall of rocks. The pain was instant, with the taste of blood almost immediately penetrating my mouth. Blood began draining from the back of my head and my hand quickly jerked to the location of the blood, and the pain. I looked at my hand. It was covered with blood, with each fingerprint showing the outline of my injury, and if there was one thing that I wasn't prepared for on this trip, that would be any form of a medical emergency.

My camera bag lay by my side, and I remembered the red bandanna that I had packed in a side compartment, something to protect my camera in times of inclement conditions.

I had also brought a bottle of cold water. I soaked the bandanna and applied pressure to the back of my head. I moved my eyes around to try to determine why I had fallen back. I noticed that one of the rocks along the bottom of the altar had been pushed out of place, sticking out a bit from its original position.

Great! I thought. *One thousand years of history and I ruin it on my first day here.* I looked around, finding that I was the only person that had noticed my fall and the stone's movement, and at this moment the pulsing pain was a secondary issue to the damaged wall.

The rock protruded out from its original location at the altar wall's base about six inches or so, like a wooden Jenga piece sticking out at the beginning of a new game. The rock was noticeably out of place, and I was thinking that I should just push it back in. The bandanna was laid across the camera bag and my hands were free to push the rock back. With all of the strength I could manage I pushed, and it didn't work. It was as if it had been pushed by me from a loose state and now wedged into a more permanent position.

Still sitting on the ground, I rotated my body facing the corner and pressed my feet against the rock, hoping that my leg strength could do the job that my hands were not able to do. The altar stood what I thought was about twelve to fifteen feet tall, and the thought flashed through my mind to just leave it alone. But in my stubbornness I was determined to fix my faux pas. The pressure of my feet against the rock increased without much change. The anxiety in my mind increased with each passing moment—I was so sure that at any moment a visitor, or worse yet, a park official, would arrive.

Finally, in a desperate attempt to shove the stone back into place I recoiled my legs and then thrust my feet back toward the stone with all the force that I could muster. My thighs recoiled and lunged at the wall. The rock exploded in two pieces, with the face of the rock falling five feet away. Terror ran through my veins.

I quickly moved to the broken piece to try to put it back in place. The smooth surface of the large and broken stone seemed strange as I lifted it off the ground. Not only was it lighter than I had expected, but it had broken off with a straight line cut around the edge. Turning the rock over, I saw that it had been hollowed out, and my head turned toward the piece remaining wedged inside the altar. It had been hollowed out as well.

I ran my fingers over the edge of the face of the rock, amazed at the clean way in which it broke open. I placed my hand in the hollowed out rock and felt something lying inside. At first, I was sure that a piece of the rock or mortar had fallen in. It felt different than I imagined, and I removed my hand and discovered a medallion, a metal pendant of sorts.

It was circular, about four inches across, and resembled a pendant worn around the neck of a king. In its center a large X made up most of the design, with a small red gemstone inlaid in the bottom corner. I rubbed off the age and dust and read an inscription that rounded the bronze medallion... *Thame aira.*

Along the edge the pendant had various grooves, creating smaller and larger gaps that created a Morse code look. The other thing I realized about the medallion: it had been placed there—it had been hidden.

Chapter 8

I walked slowly with the medallion hidden away deep in my camera bag. The altar rock was still out of place, but I found a tube of Superglue, which I had used in emergency situations to hold fabric or a prop into its place, in one of the compartments of my camera bag and glued it back into place. Never had I found an emergency situation so fitting.

With no one to witness the act, I thought it best to move along and discover the rest of Battle and its surrounding areas. It wasn't until I got behind the wheel of my car that I was finally able to relax; the adrenaline finally slowed down, but with the energy boost that had made me forget about my head, a headache followed. My finger ran across to the area of the injury and the wound seemed to have stopped bleeding.

Pevensey and Battle was much better training ground for my driving skills than London. My Jetta made its way through the narrow streets, while I looked for a drug store to buy something for the pain and maybe a restroom to clean up in.

On the edge of town appeared a historical monument sign— Battle Baths—written in ancient Roman script. I turned in. This was an area of English history that had failed to capture my imagination, but with the site right in front of me I couldn't resist.

I picked up a brochure, choosing that over the iPod rental that provided a step-by-step tour of the grounds.

As I turned the first corner into the grounds, I noticed a familiar figure positioned in the floor of a tiled bath area. Her hair was pulled back in a loose ponytail pulling it up to her mid back –it was Gabriela. I removed my camera from its bag and approached the edge of the back wall.

"Ciao!" I said.

She looked at me, either surprised to hear Italian, or because someone had actually spoken to her.

"Hey there, what are you doing here?" she asked in Italian.

"Slow down…In English, please." I smiled. "I only know a couple words, including Andrea Bocelli!" I replied.

"Oh, sorry." Gabriela stood up. I couldn't help but notice her body. It was obvious that Gabriela took care of herself. Her fitted black Under Armor pullover and black Capri's showed off a body fit and trim. "What are you doing here?" she questioned.

"Well, I was driving by looking for a drugstore and saw the marker, so I thought I would stop in," I answered.

"Isn't it amazing?" she responded. "Two thousand years of craftsmanship almost completely intact."

"I am starting to see how you fell in love with this stuff," I answered.

"These tiles that line the floor were brought in from Sicily, hand-crafted individually, painted and fired. Could you imagine what something like that would cost today?" she said.

"I can only imagine," I replied.

"So what about you? Did you find anything this morning?" she asked.

The events of the morning flashed through my mind quickly, and I was unsure about how to answer. "Well, let's just say that things really opened up for me," I said smiling. I then reached my hand down to help Gabriela up the stairs. Her hands felt firm with long, strong fingers—but with soft skin—as she grabbed my hand to pull herself up the last stair.

"So how is your morning in an ancient bathhouse coming along?" I asked.

"It has been wonderful. Come with me and let me show you something."

Gabriela walked quickly ahead of me, showing me through the various parts of this Roman bathhouse that had remained as well as it had for almost two thousand years.

"I wanted to show you this," she said.

"It looks like some kind of stall or something," I said.

"Exactly! This is the locker room, not that much different from something you would see in use today in a gym," she told me while pointing to the ancient locker room.

"So who would use a place like this?" I asked.

"Well, first of all, only three other locations survived in this condition from the Roman Empire, but this was typically a place for Roman officials, officers and members of the legion. With this location so close to the ships coming from all over the kingdom, many naval officers came here to relax and cleanup, so to speak."

I admired the passion with which Gabriela spoke, and her independence in coming here alone to discover more of her passion. She told me of the history of the bathhouses, the architectural creations, the water source, the water itself, and the plumbing required to keep a facility like this in operation, and how the water temperature was altered. I took pictures as she talked, of the two thousand year old painted tiles, the columns, and her.

"How much longer are you going to be here?" I asked.

"Well, I was planning on leaving tomorrow and heading to Bognor Regis, down the coast," she said.

"What about for today? Are you taking some time to grab some lunch?" I asked.

"I was going to eventually," she said.

"Well, I need to talk to someone. I stumbled into something," I said.

Gabriela looked puzzled. "Stumbled?" she asked.

"How about we go find some of those famous fish and chips that I've heard so much about?" I asked.

"I went to a great place yesterday, not too far from here. Are you driving?" she asked.

"Only if I have to!" I smiled.

"Deal," she responded.

"King's Fish House" was painted on the front door window of an older building located just off the main street through Battle. I pulled the door open and the bell rang as Gabriela and I walked into an aroma that made me think of Boston. The smell of saltwater, fish, and oil made my stomach growl and my mouth water. Above the counter, a simple hand-crafted sign said it all.

Fish and chips 7 pounds 50 showing. Fish chowder 3 pounds per cup.

"Seems pretty simple," I said looking at the sign.

"It is delicious. I tried the chowder yesterday," Gabriela said, rubbing her hands together.

"Afternoon, folks. What can we get for ya?" said a short man who had come to the counter, after having had his back to us initially while stirring a pot filled with the fish chowder. He was a man in his sixties, standing about 5 feet 6 inches, with a large stomach held together, it seemed, by a white apron that looked like it hadn't been washed in a few days, or weeks.

"How about your fish and chips for me, and…" I paused, looking at Gabriela.

"Me too," she answered.

We sat in the corner of the small diner and began eating our lunch. Ketchup was nowhere to be found, but a bottle of malt vinegar sat between our two plates.

"So what is this mystery that you came to stumble upon?" Gabriela asked, then threw a deep-fried potato in her mouth. I had felt comfortable with Gabriela from the beginning, and I felt like I could trust her with the events that had occurred earlier in the morning.

"Well, I found something." I leaned over to the camera bag that hadn't left my side since leaving Battle Mount. I sat up straight and brought my hands up in front of my face, placing the medallion between my thumb and index finger. "I found this," I said.

Gabriela's eyes widened for a moment, examining the circular object from a distance, and then she answered. "I've seen that before," she said, and then took a bite of her cod.

Chapter 9

Gabriela began.

"Just down the coast from here is Bognor Regis, a place that I was heading to tomorrow. It was an extremely important settlement beginning in the first century as a port for shipping out most of the ores and goods what were mined in southern England. Early Roman armies had positioned a large garrison there to protect the lead and tin going out to Rome and the wine and olive oil coming in."

"In 1976, an excavation was begun by the British National Archives after a fisherman found a chest located near the coastline filled with early Roman coinage from the third century, gold Spanish doubloons from about 1550 and other miscellaneous things of value. The chest was discovered buried along the bank, and seemed to have been unearthed partially by a large rainstorm that had torn away a portion of the steep embankment. Archeologists discovered the burned buried remains of an ancient Roman warehouse and financial office used to settle transactions of all incoming and outgoing shipments."

I sat in amazement eating my fish as she continued.

"There is a legend of Caratacus, who would have been the William Wallace of his time. Caratacus was a tribal chieftain near Wales. Many of the Roman soldiers upon completion of their thirty years of service to the Roman legion were given freedom and the promise of their own land grants in various veterans' colonies.

Caratacus wasn't happy with the arrangements. Those lands given to the soldiers would be taken directly from the local Britons, so he engaged in some of the first known examples of guerrilla warfare, striking at the troops of Emperor Claudius at a moment's notice, only to disappear into the trees or countryside, almost like ghosts. Caratacus had found out about a larger shipment of coins sent by Claudius as a reward for the outlaw. As the chariot with the treasury was traveling to London, Caratacus and his close unit of henchmen attacked the caravan, killing everyone and riding off with about ten thousand pieces of silver. Most of those coins were never accounted for. So in 1976, when the large trunk was finally opened, included in it was about five thousand Roman coins, one thousand Spanish doubloons, and an unusually oversized medallion, marked with only a large X in the middle and a series of notches and grooves that move around the outside exactly like the one you have in your hand right now; only part of the top was broke off."

"Is it exactly the same?" I asked.

Gabriela held up her finger, asking for a minute to finally chew the food that had started to cool off in front of her. "Sorry," I added, smiling at her, realizing I was almost finished, and she had barely begun to eat.

"I have a photograph of it in some of my research of Bognor on my laptop," she said.

"Do you know where it is located now?" I asked.

"The British Museum of History in London, I would suppose," she answered.

The smell of leather seats filled my rented Jetta as we sat quietly in the parking lot for the bathhouses.

"What are you going to do now?" Gabriela asked

"Well, I would love to know what is known about the medallion that was found. Where it is? What it was for and who was it that owned it?" I answered.

"Let's look at the images of the one that they found in Bognor," she said.

We found a picnic table and Gabriela booted up her laptop. After finding the folder of Bognor Regis, she located the images of the matching medallion.

"See, it is identical! Only the one you hold is in perfect shape. The one found in the chest had most of the top broken off," Gabriela said with an air of enthusiasm.

"Is there a way to zoom in on the image, toward the bottom?" I asked. If there was one thing I had discovered about my creative brain as a photographer, it was my attention to the details in others photographs. Like the time my colleague Ann shot a series of photographs while at a Red Sox game with some friends at Fenway Park to see the Sox. One of her photos contained a background image of a fan trying to catch a foul ball while holding two large beers, failing miserably. The beer was splashed all over him, and the ball had bounced up hitting him in the face and leaving him with a grimace of pain. I had noticed that almost immediately, and the photo became a favorite on www.awkwardphotomoments.com.

As Gabriela zoomed in, the details of the image became clearer, including the same gemstone that was set in "my" medallion, only the photographed medallion's gem was set deep center on the bottom, whereas mine was to the right of the bottom.

The captioning on the photo read "THAME AIRA COIN, British Museum of Ancient History."

"If this is a coin, then its value is X, which would be equal to ten. But ten of what?" I tried to surmise, with limited language skills.

"The writing is not Latin, or Spanish, or anything else that I've studied. I would only imagine that it is an older form of English or Old English," Gabriela responded.

"The River Thames includes an 's' that isn't included here, so could you imagine someone taking the time to create this beautiful coin, only to misspell a word on it? And what about the gemstone? Is that a normal feature on a coin?" I asked with a furrowed brow.

Gabriela started to type quickly into Google, "Thame Aira Coin." The search only brought up ten results. "The first one is the British Museum of Ancient History," she said. Then with her own look of confusion she added, "Page not found," after she had clicked on the link. We continued looking at each of the results and found that there was no information online, on any site, relating to the "Thame Aira Coin."

"That is so strange," I remarked. Gabriela searched the records of the Web site for the British Museum of Ancient History. The "Contact Us" page was found, and I dialed the number.

"Hello. How are you? Good. I am looking for an item in the museum. It's called the 'Thame Aira Coin.' Yes, I can. T-H-A-M-E-A-I-R-A," I said, spelling it out for them. "That's right. Are you sure? Well, does it say anything else? OK, well thank you." I hung up the phone.

"What was said?" Gabriela inquired.

"Well, he said that there was no image listed in their current inventory database, but the thing that was strange was that he did show a listing for a 'Thame Era Coin,' but the entry for it said 'No Longer Listed.' It had been deleted. Where did you get the image on your laptop?" I asked.

"Il mio professore shared with us the images. He had been part of the dig team in Bognor," she answered.

"Is there any way to talk to him?" I asked.

"Unfortunately, he passed away a few years ago. I just remember his details of the dig. Not so much of the artifacts, but more of the built structures," she replied.

"Some help you are!" I joked, smiling.

"So now what?" she asked.

I ran my fingers across my upper chin, trying to think of my next move. "I have no idea." I explained to Gabriela about the reason that the trip had been planned, and how Monica had wanted this as much as I did, but for completely different reasons. I told her enough information so that she could understand, but not too much to overwhelm her with my life story. I continued that I was using the bed-and-breakfast vouchers, and my trip was not structured at all.

"There is a small site museum in Bognor. I was heading there next, so maybe you can get some answers there?" she told me.

I stared off in the distance, almost in a trance. I thought about this moment, with the unknown treasure and a beautiful woman, and the dream of my childhood of always wanting to find something of historical value. I thought about Battle and how I wanted to show Gabriela the altar wall and the place of the medallion. But it would be too risky. What if someone had seen me?

"What are you thinking?" Gabriela asked as she studied my facial expressions.

"Come with me," I answered.

Gabriela sat for a brief moment, staring off herself.

"Come with me to Bognor and let's see if we can come up with any answers. If we can't, then at least we tried. I can do some detective work while you research your ruins. After that, you can continue on your way and me on mine. I was planning on hitting Stonehenge, then on to Bath and Glastonbury, and who knows from there. I would love some companionship. What do you say?" I asked in a bold yet non-begging way. "I could serve as your personal photographer."

Gabriela laughed. "Sei matta (*You are crazy*)."

⁓

There was something about Jonah that seemed to be drawing her to him. She thought back to earlier in the morning, about how she saw him from over her newspaper; his hair was a mess, and he was trying to push it down with his hands. He seemed very innocent, harmless.

⁓

"I would love to. But, what should I do with my car? I have to return it tomorrow," she told me, spinning the car key chain on her long fingers.

"We can return it now and see if they will give you a refund. Unlikely, but we can try," I answered.

I pulled up next to the driver's side door of Gabriela's small Honda. In my thoughts about her, the medallion, and tomorrow, I had forgotten about the driver's door being on the opposite side of the car. Gabriela opened her door, taking with her the laptop bag, and walked around to the front of the Jetta. I got out opening her car door.

"So, I will meet you back at the house?" I asked.

"Si," she said, lightly punching me in the shoulder.

"Are you going to need help finding it?" I joked.

"No, but I will need something else," Gabriela responded.

"What is that?" I asked.

"Someone to fix my car. Both of the tires on this side have been slashed," she responded.

Chapter 10

The hour-and-a-half drive from Battle to Bognor Regis took much longer than we had anticipated. The sun had not set when we left, and was still perched in the sky beautifully over the Atlantic, but then it slowly began its descent, almost as if the curtain of the Globe Theater coming down on the first act of Shakespeare's King Lear; the water seemed to be on fire.

Gabriela and I took our time, stopping at various sites along the way, including a few castle remains, the great Arundel Castle, and a roadside stand near Brighton that was selling freshly picked berries. We talked and laughed and got to know each other. It felt normal for me. This had always been my strength.

Gabriela told me about growing up on the outskirts of Rome, about her mathematician father, Benicio, who worked for a think tank based there, and about her mother, Bella, who grew up in Tuscany on her father's olive farm. Gabriela had grown up the youngest of four children with her three older brothers, with her father and especially her mother treating her as their most precious gift.

Growing up, Gabriela had been protected from all of the men and boys by her older brothers. She looked like her mother, and by the age of fifteen she was known all around as the most beautiful girl in school. Her father had worked hard to teach her mathematics, and she loved algebra, geometry, and calculus and excelled in all other subjects as well. As a twelve year old girl, her father had taken her to visit the Coliseum. Benicio had spent the afternoon with Gabriela, while her brothers were watching as Roma squared off against AC Milan in a football match. He explained mathematics in terms of architecture; how the building was constructed and how math was used in its design. This stuck with Gabby, as her father called her when they were alone. Her focus became architecture and she dove into her studies, preparing for university. She took Latin, Greek, and even Hebrew to try to fully become prepared for various words used in the field.

Then at the University of Rome, she took a class that changed her life: Roman Architecture in the Age of Empire. She dreaded going home to tell her father of her desire to change her focus, moving to the study of ancient Roman architecture. She wanted to work, teach, and research architecture from a historical perspective.

It had broken her father's heart, although he never said anything, but she could just see it in his countenance. Her mother told her not to worry about it. All that mattered was what made Gabriela happy; her father would get over his issues.

Her mother had taught Gabriela how to cook classic Italian dishes, something that she spent her time doing when she wasn't on the road. I wondered about a few other details, including her age, which I figured was somewhere between twenty-eight and thirty-four, and her relationship, or lack of one. She wore no ring; I had gathered that pretty early on.

A comfortable silence had set in, and the thought of the medallion and its inscription rested on my mind, and the language that it was written in. What was it?

"Could you do me a favor?" I asked.

"Sure," Gabriela replied.

"Could you write down some letters for me?" I answered back, with a writing motion from my hand that I freed from the steering wheel. Gabriela found a tablet and pen in her bag and wrote as I said, "A-I-R-A-T-H-A-M-E. It just doesn't make any sense. Why would someone go through all the trouble to create two medallions of such detailed workmanship, only to misspell the words?"

"What if it's not a coin?" she asked. "What does the X stand for?"

"X marks the spot. Ten." I added sarcastically.

"In Greek, X stands for Christ, as in Jesus Christ. You know, like X-mas," Gabriela said.

I paused and pulled off the side of the road slowly. "Are you OK?" she asked looking at me inquisitorially.

I slowly turned toward Gabriela and said, "Write these letters down please. A-R-I-M-A-T-H-E-A."

"OK, now what?" she said.

"Now mark off each common letter between our two lists and see if there are any letters left," I responded looking straight ahead.

"They match!" she squealed, almost as if she had won the lottery.

I began to tell her what I knew.

"As legend tells it, Joseph of Arimathea was a high-ranking member of the Sanhedrin, and some even believe that he was the uncle of Jesus Christ. Joseph's occupation was that of a dealer of ore, tin and lead here in England. There are stories of Jesus traveling with him to England during his late teens or twenties; in fact, there is a hymn, "Jerusalem," which makes that claim. After the crucifixion, Jesus was laid in a tomb, a tomb given by Joseph of Arimathea. After the crucifixion, it is believed that Joseph took with him at least two items from Jerusalem here to England, near Glastonbury: the cup from the Last Supper, and the crown of thorns from Christ's head. Those thorns from the hawthorn bush, or a remnant of the bush, used to create the crown of thorns Jesus wore were wrapped around the walking staff of Joseph as a reminder. Upon arriving in Glastonbury, legend has it that Joseph thrust his staff into the ground and it took root. Ironically, that particular variety of bush only grows in the Middle East, but there is one bush that grows near the abbey at Glastonbury. I was planning on going there to look around during my visit."

"So two medallions are found hidden in Southern England, bearing the name of Jesus and his alleged uncle, each with a gemstone, and the only one known to the public has been deleted from the museum database. What do you think that this all means?" Gabriela tried to surmise.

"I have no idea, but I will think better with a full stomach," I answered back with a laugh. We drove into a very quiet Bognor Regis and I pulled the car slowly into a parking lot next to a restaurant, The Squawking Chicken, and looked at Gabriela.

"Are you hungry?" I asked.

"I could eat something, I suppose," she said as she was deep in thought.

The Squawking Chicken was a quaint little Chinese restaurant not far from the picturesque coast of England. Not much else seemed to be open in Bognor at this time of night. As we had driven through slowly we noticed that most of the shops had closed, with only a pub and the restaurant having any signs of life.

The waitress arrived at our table asking if there was anything that we needed. I asked only for a glass of ice water and Gabriela a glass of wine. I asked Ming, our waitress, how the name of the restaurant had originated. Laughing, she started.

"Da owna of rstrnt when brn cryd all da time. Said he sound like a squawking chikn. Name kind of stuck," she said.

Suddenly a voice rang out from the back of the kitchen, "Moo goo gai pan, order up!." Gabriela and I laughed. "I see what you mean," Gabriela remarked.

"That not even him, that his son," she giggled.

For the next hour, Gabriela and I shared an order of chicken chow mein and the Queen's Chicken, a local favorite that Queen Elizabeth had allegedly eaten on a trip through Bognor in the early '70s, shortly after the Squawking Chicken opened.

I pulled out a pen and scribbled some notes on a napkin. "So what do we know?" I said, sounding a lot like a Boston cop on the scene of a dead body.

"Two coins, both hidden in two separate locations along the southern coast of England. One at the site of the invasion of William the Conqueror and the other found along with other things buried at the site of an ancient Roman port. Both coins reference an unknown language, or possibly contain a reference to Jesus Christ and/or Joseph of Arimathea. Both are identical, with the only difference being the placement of a gemstone. Your thoughts?" I asked.

"Well, maybe we can get some answers at the museum in the morning," Gabriela said, with a look of needing to relax and get some sleep.

I had called Dottie's Inn while Gabriela had excused herself from the table at dinner. Dottie met us at the door welcoming us in.

Gabriela glanced over toward me as I opened the Jetta getting the luggage out of the back. She had only met me 15 hours ago. Was she crazy? Was I crazy to invite someone I barely knew to come on a trip with me?

"Good evening, folks. Welcome to Dottie's. I am Dottie. Did you find it OK?"

"Good evening. Yes we did, thank you," I responded.

"I'll let you get to your room now. Right this way," she replied.

Dottie opened the door to a large room, with a queen-size bed, small closet, dresser, and a bathroom, all decorated as if it came directly from a Thomas Kinkade painting. The addition to the room was an old fashioned cot already set up against the wall shared with the entry door.

"Just as you asked for," Dottie said winking at me, smiling slightly. "Breakfast will be ready at 8:00 am, unless you would like it earlier?"

I looked at Gabriela. "Eight o'clock would be perfect. Thank you."

I quickly changed into a pair of shorts and a T-shirt, realizing that through the events of the day I had forgotten to check the back of my head and my wound. The blood had dried and had been camouflaged by the darkness of my dark brown hair, or at least that is what I supposed. Gabriela hadn't said anything about it.

I sat down on my cot and pulled out my laptop and typed an email to a friend of mine at Boston University in their history department asking him if there was any information that he could come up with in regards to the medallion. I had avoided my instincts as a photographer to take pictures of everything. The last thing that I had wanted to happen to me at Battle was to have been stopped and questioned with images of the altar wall and the broken rock on my camera. I thought about the trusting soul that Gabriela must be to believe me from the beginning, not being able to go back to the location at Battle Mount.

The door opened from the bathroom, and emerging from it was Gabriela wearing a satin pajama set that clung to her body, like it was full of static electricity. Her hair was loosely pulled over her left shoulder, and she was smiling.

"It's all yours," Gabriela said walking across the room.

"Thanks. I just need to brush my teeth."

Gabriela was applying lotion to her feet when I came out. "My feet are killing me," she said.

"Can I?" I asked, moving closer to her.

"I guess we are sharing the same room," she joked with a smile.

I moved a chair from the corner of the room to the side of the bed, and Gabriela sat with her arms wrapped around her knees, which had been pulled up against her chest. My hands gently pulled her feet toward me resting them on my lap. I starting rubbing them with my fingers.

"Inter. Mio Dio! Mamma mia! That feels so good."

Gabriela fell back lying on the bed, putting her hands over her eyes. After finishing her feet, I moved my hands up rubbing her calves, hearing now only an occasional soft sound of approval. My mind was torn between the legs of Gabriela, her stomach that was exposed slightly from her hands resting comfortably above her head, and the day in the rear view mirror and what could be on the horizon for tomorrow.

"Che così si sente bene." sleepily came from Gabriela's lips.

I realized that she had fallen asleep. I found an extra blanket on the closet shelf and covered her, not wanting to wake her up. I looked across the room, eying my six-foot cot awaiting my six-foot-four-inch body. I couldn't wait. I lay unable to sleep for another hour.

Chapter 11

The year was 1295 A.D. and the earth was still flat.

The castle at Tewkesbury stood quiet. The mid-September warm afternoon had an eerie blanket of calm laying over the entire estate.

For the casual observer it would have been hard to distinguish whether this visual scene was real life, or a picturesque scene hung on a wall, but the muted sounds of a bird chirping served as a reminder of life.

Two women emerged from the back of the estate carrying a rug rolled up to the area designated for carpet cleaning, or carpet beating, as it were. The colorfully woven rugs of reds, blacks and greens exhaled breaths of dirt and dust, coughing out with each swing of the wooden rug paddles, reminiscent of two modern-day lumberjacks, taking turns swinging their axes as the forest tree readies to fall.

Matilda walked down a quiet hall carrying a neatly folded armload of freshly washed sheets and blankets. She had ordered the housekeepers out to clean the rugs, James, the estate's "I will take care of it man," down to the market to pick up a few supplies, and

Mary, her assistant, down to the kitchen to bring up a basin full of warm water.

Matilda stood at the doorway one last time, stopping to listen; she heard nothing. A deafening quiet echoed silence through the stone-walled castle, if that was possible. Matilda's hand grabbed ahold of the door's handle and slowly but confidently entered into Joan's bedroom. Joan of Acre was about to give birth, but did not display any signs of a woman already dilated to six centimeters. She smiled as Matty (the name Joan had used to refer to Matilda) entered the room and said, with a hint of restrained pain, "Did you get the linens?" while breathing out sharply.

"Yes I did, my lady," Matty answered, placing the linens on the chair at the foot of the blanket stripped bed. "Mary will be up momentarily with the water."

"Please, enough of the 'lady.' You know I want you to call me Joan," Lady De Clare answered back.

A sharp pain struck Joan. Her hands grabbed the sheets tightly with her fingers.

"It won't be long," Matty answered while she pushed up Joan's flowing skirt.

This was the scene that was now in its fourth act. Matty had been present and in charge of Joan's previous three births, preparing for each with meticulous detail and care. It had become second nature now for Matty, who had been Joan's handmaid over the previous seven years, since Joan had married Gilbert de Clare, one of England's most wealthy and powerful men. Gilbert had given Matilda to Joan before their wedding, and Joan and Matty had hit it off from the beginning.

Matty's mother had provided similar services for Gilbert's first wife, and he knew that Matty would be trained the right way. Matilda had learned everything that there was to know about running a household, from the rest of the service staff, the education of the children, but especially her place as a confidante, not a friend. She had shrugged off the desires of Joan for her to drop the naming formalities, but Matty had insisted. Matty believed that with Joan's standing as the lady of the house, wife of the Duke of Clare, and as the daughter of King Edward (Longshanks) and Queen Isabella of England, she deserved respect, but more importantly at this time, dignity.

Matty thought back to Joan's first and second births and the screams and wailings that accompanied each. She remembered how the sounds of each birth echoed through the cold castle's stone anti-acoustical walls, and how many of the servants had thought Lady Joan was dying. It wouldn't happen this time; she had sent the staff out, the three older children were out being taught Latin, Gilbert was away on one of his normal birthing trips, and Joan's third birth had been much quieter.

A sheet had been laid under the bed perpendicular to its length, then brought up and tied loosely around Joan's wrists, allowing her to grab and pull against its own tightness when it was time to push. A cool wet cloth was applied to Joan's forehead once Mary had returned back to the room from the kitchen with the water.

"It's coming!" Joan groaned as her knees were brought up allowing her to push harder.

"Breath, my lady. It will be over soon enough," Matty quietly pleaded.

Joan took in a few more deep breaths and pushed again.

"One more and the babe will be here!" Matty exclaimed. And with that command, almost as if she were a conductor organizing and leading an orchestra, Matty took the baby from Joan's womb, tied and cut the umbilical cord and washed it in the tub of warm water.

"It is a girl, my lady. It is a girl!" Matty excitedly announced.

Mary sat in horror and wonder, having witnessed a child's birth for the first time. Matty had confidence in the young fifteen-year-old Mary, knowing this would begin the next chapter of her training as a royal handmaid.

Matty carefully wrapped the infant into a blanket and placed her into Joan's awaiting arms. The baby's small, delicate fingers, fragile body, and angelic face looked entirely like her mother, and nothing like her red-haired, burly father.

"We shall call her Elizabeth," Joan whispered softly. That began the life of Elizabeth de Clare, on September 16, 1295. The day the earth was still flat.

Chapter 12

The smell of perfume brought my senses to life. I awoke after a mostly sleepless night and found myself lying on the floor, having moved off the cot at some point in the middle of the night.

The bed that had been occupied by Gabriela was empty and made; the blanket that I had used to cover her, folded in the empty chair in the corner. The clock on the wall said 7:15 a.m., and a noise came from the bathroom. I sat up and noticed a slight crack in the door, with Gabriela standing in front of the mirror performing her morning ritual, wearing a large towel wrapped around her body and a lot of hair. My own noise caused Gabriela to look at the reflection in the mirror at me; she smiled, noticing that I had been watching her.

"Buona mattina, Jonah," she said in a sing-song voice.

"Good morning to you," I responded while running my fingers through my hair. The bathroom door opened and she walked toward me, kissing me on the cheek.

"What was that for?" I questioned, wondering about how to get more of the same treatment.

"Last night. Thank you for rubbing my feet and for the blanket. It really felt so good. I am so sorry that I fell asleep," she responded.

"No worries, I could tell that you were tired, but you are welcome," I replied back.

"I will be out of your way in just a bit. I promise," she said, leaning back into the mirror and applying mascara to her eyes.

"Don't worry about that. The museum doesn't open for another few hours. We have plenty of time," I said.

I jumped in the shower, and the hot water felt good running through my hair and down my body. The dark-colored water reminded me of my head wound, and the cut stung a bit as I shampooed. I wrapped myself in a towel and realized that my pants were left on my luggage in the room, so I called through the door to Gabriela. No answer. The door to the bedroom was cracked and Gabriela was nowhere to be found. I walked out, and as I stood holding my pants in one hand, I heard the door open behind me to the hallway.

"I am so sorry. I guess I should have knocked," she said holding a bag of fruit in one hand and her sunglasses in the other. "I just went out to grab some breakfast."

"I'll be right back," I said, shutting the door behind me and seeing that Gabriela was watching me, too.

"So what is the first thing on the agenda for the day?" Gabriela asked as we sat on the bed eating the varieties of fruit that lay in front of us.

"Well, I would love to go visit the Bognor Dig Museum," I responded. "What about you? What would you like to do? Anything or any place you have in mind?"

"I would love to go up to Salisbury. There is a great example of a Roman iron works there," she said with an air of excitement, wanting to show me a part of her world.

The breakfast was completed and I asked Gabriela if we should just use Dottie's as the room for the next night as well. "I think that would work," she replied.

It was a short drive to the Bognor museum. I felt as excited to be there with Gabriela as I was to be in England itself with everything going on around us. Her presence had reminded me of the best of times in my life, those years of being married and the magical few months with Monica. Gabriela sat comfortably in the passenger's seat with her legs crossed, showing the long, lean tone of her legs. She smelled wonderful, I thought to myself. I had remembered hearing somewhere about Italian women and their beauty secret of using lemons and olive oil on their hair and skin. Whatever Gabriela was doing, it was working well. My driving had finally become somewhat comfortable, even if I was sitting on the wrong side of the car, driving on the wrong side of the road.

Gabriela reached in the backseat to get her sunglasses out of her bag. The sun had risen, and as we drove almost directly into the morning light it was hard to see. With her glasses in place and her right arm resting on the console separating us, Gabriela's hand brushed up against mine. Her hand adjusted again, this time wrapping her pinkie around mine. Blood rushed through my body, seemingly all depositing in my face.

The initial brush of Gabriela's hand was enough to cause my heart to skip a beat, and this interaction brought back memories of twenty years before, when I was a seventeen-year-old high school senior finally holding my girlfriend's hand for the first time. I remembered that well. Never in my early life had I shown affection to a girl, until that day when me and my only high school girlfriend, Carla, held hands for the first time. It was almost like a contest as we walked next to each other down the hall, seeing how close our hands could get without actually touching, with each stride getting closer and closer. Then finally the collision happened, wrapping our fingers inside and around each other's opposite hand. The rush of emotions and feelings overcame me then, and started once again now.

Gabriela glanced at me, pulling her glasses to the end of her nose. "Are you OK? she asked.

"I'm better than OK," I said, taking her hand completely into mine.

The Bognor Museum opened at 9:30 am. It was built inside a completely restored Roman administrative office building. A partial fresco had been brought into the museum depicting Neptune, the Roman god of water, and they had placed it on the wall behind the reception desk that housed the employee on duty. The desk had a variety of postcards, books, and DVD's for sale, and even a series of Bognor collectible plates and spoons.

"Morning, folks!" came the voice of an elderly gentleman from behind the counter.

"Good morning. How are you?" Gabriela echoed back, with a thicker accent than what I had heard from her at this point.

"A beautiful summer morning along the greatest coastline in the world!" he laughed. "What can we do for you today? You two look like you are on a mission for something."

"What can you tell us about the dig here in 1976?" I asked.

"Well, first of all, allow me to introduce myself to my foreign visitors; a beautiful Italian and a bloody Yank, I presume?" he said with a laugh.

We both nodded. "Gabriela and Jonah," I answered.

"Piers Waite is my name. The dig of '76. Well, it was in early spring, and a local fisherman was heading down to the beach to do some clamming. There had been a massive spring storm that had swept ashore from the Atlantic, and as he made his way down the trail, he saw the remains of a bank that had washed out, like a mudslide. As he took a closer look, the remains of a wall had been uncovered by the movement of the dirt bank. Local officials called the Archeology Department at the University of Bath, who came down and began a fifteen month excavation, mostly finding this fresco you see behind me, along with some Roman tools and a couple trunks that had been hidden beneath a trap door in the floor of the place."

"Do you know what they found in the trunks?" I asked.

"Well, yes I do. We have some of the stuff on display, and back here in the side room are some of the samples," he said while leading us down a short corridor into a mostly Roman-style room filled with tools for a garden, pottery pieces, a small hand mirror, and a large glass case displaying Roman coins from circa 100 AD.

"I have heard from a professor that they also uncovered some other coins, namely Spanish doubloons," Gabriela said.

"Well, yes they did. No one seemed to know exactly where they came from. Parliament had passed the Antiquities Act in 1973, making all antiques and finds property of the Crown. They gave the local historical board a choice of so many items to keep for display once a museum was finished. The board felt that with the ancient history of the Roman influence here, the logical things to choose from the find would be things of a Roman nature," Piers answered.

"Was there anything else? Any other coins found?" I asked.

Piers thought for a moment. "Well, yes. Part of that Antiquities Act was a "first choice" clause, giving whoever located the treasure first choice as a finder's fee, so to speak. Jimmy Keepe was the finder, and he chose to keep a much larger, damaged coin. One that was damaged! Didn't make a damn bit of sense to me; to any of us, for that matter!" he replied with a hint of frustration.

"Why not?" Gabriela asked.

"There was just so much stuff. So many beautiful undamaged coins," he said as he pointed across to the glass cabinet. "But he chose one that was broken."

"Does he still have it?" I asked.

"He doesn't talk about it anymore," he answered.

"Do you think it would be possible to speak to him?" Gabriela asked.

"We are doing a bit of research about it," I included.

"Jimmy is a tough nut to crack. He keeps to himself these days. Doesn't get out for much of anything," he replied.

"Could you tell us how we could get ahold of him?" I asked.

"Let me phone him. I'll be right back." Piers walked away slowly toward the main hall. Gabriela looked at me.

"It seems that we are making some progress. Don't you think?" she remarked.

"Yes. It is just so hard to believe that twenty-four hours ago I had that thing in my hand, and now here we stand. Not sure what to even think," I said as Piers entered the room again.

"It took a little prodding, but he agreed to talk to you, on one condition. You never use his name," Piers announced.

"Deal," I said.

Jimmy Keepe was a funny looking eighty-year-old man, not more than five feet six inches, barely a tooth in his mouth and a full head of white hair. His oversized khaki trousers were cinched together tightly at his waist by a belt with its excess length hanging down by his side. A yellow fisherman hat, flannel shirt, and rubber boots completed his ensemble. Jimmy had also agreed to meet us for lunch, if we bought. He had recommended the South Shore Tavern, a place that Gabriela and I discovered was more known for free food with purchased pints of Guinness.

"Mr. Keepe, thank you for agreeing to meet with us," I started out the conversation.

"Jimmy. Please call me Jimmy. I haven't been asked about this in a long time," he responded

Gabriela looked at him. "What can you tell us about your coin? Do you have it with you?"

"Bloody hell. No! They took it!" Jimmy finished with a slap on the table, then a quick mouthful of Guinness.

"Who took it?" I asked.

"The government, someone from the government. In 1986 I got a call from somebody in Buckingham Palace, asking me if they could come down and look at my coin. I couldn't exactly say no. Later that day, these two guys come up to me house down by the docks, all wearing black suits and such. They told me they needed to look at my coin, so I got it out of my hiding spot. They looked at it for a few minutes, looking at it with some kind of eyepiece. They sat my coin down and I walked over to pick it back up, and then they stopped me.

They said, "Mr. Keepe, what you have here is an item of extreme national simportance. This coin needs to be kept safe, and by order of the Queen herself we must take it into our possession at once."

I said to them, "But I have it hidden...it was my reward."

"We understand that, Mr. Keepe. Her Majesty's government is prepared to compensate you. We have for you a bank check in the amount of five thousand pounds, and of course the thanks of Her Majesty Queen Elizabeth II."

"They asked me not to mention it to anyone, but that was twenty five years ago. I wished I hadn't given it to them," he said.

"Well, it doesn't sound like you had a lot of choice," I replied.

"So what brings the two of you here to ask me about my coin?" he questioned.

"Can you keep a secret?" I asked.

"Yes," he said in a hushed tone.

I replied, "I found an identical coin yesterday."

Chapter 13

The smell of the warm summer breeze off the Atlantic intoxicated me as we walked out of the pub and started the short walk down toward the Bognor pier a couple blocks away. I stepped into the crosswalk, reaching back grabbing Gabriela's hand. We walked in a comfortable silence, admiring this small oceanside town from different perspectives. Mine was a history of this place, the people who had walked over these same streets for centuries, and for Gabriela the workmanship and architectural designs of each building, both residential and commercial.

"How are you feeling about Mr. Jimmy and his story about the coin?" she asked me as we got closer to the pier.

"Very interested, to say the least. I was thinking back to our findings of it online and of it being deleted off the site. I have no reason to believe that he was lying to us," I remarked.

The long Bognor pier appeared high above the ocean surface. Gabriela and I watched as a couple of adolescents ran out toward the fading tide, only to turn, running back toward the safety of the dry sand, being chased back by the charging force of the approaching surf. Seagulls spoke to one another, eyeing the spilled popcorn kernels that lined areas of the sidewalk following the beach line.

"So Mr. Jonah, tell me more about you," Gabriela said, as if we were on our first date.

"Well, what do you want to know?" I responded.

"Kids? Do you have children? A wife? A girlfriend?" she said with a tug of my hand.

I laughed out loud, smiling after. "OK, first of all, no wife. I do have an ex-wife, but no wife. We were divorced about three years ago. Girlfriend is in the past, and I do have two kids," I remarked holding up two fingers. "Two great kids, Lilly and Dawson."

"Do you see them much?" she asked.

"Not as much as I would like." I seemed to drift off in thought for a moment.

"Sorry, have I asked something that was none of my business?" Gabriela asked with a worried expression on her face.

"No, no, not at all. I was just thinking, and realized that in all the commotion I haven't called them since I landed. I was just thinking that I need to call them tonight."

I continued on to tell Gabriela about Lilly and Dawson and about my ten year marriage to Diane, and briefly about the last three months with Monica. I mentioned my own faithfulness and left it at that. I am sure that my own uncertainty showed through as I tried to explain what life had been like for me in the last three years since the divorce, including school and work, and with that the traveling that demanded larger chunks of my time. I told her about Lilly and Dawson, how much I cared for them and loved them, and more than anything just wanted them to be happy...to be truly happy.

Gabriela's hand tightened around mine as I spoke. I felt like she could recognize in my voice the kind of person that I was. I had noticed those things about her as well.

"Gabriela de Laurentis of Rome, what would you like to share with me about you?" I asked.

"Well, I have no children, and I've never been married. Once I got out of University, I dove into my work and my career," she said.

I thought initially that she was sounding a lot like Monica.

"I kind of felt a strange pull in opposite directions, with my father and his drive for learning and a career, and my mother wanting me to find someone to settle down with and start producing grandchildren. I guess in a way, my father won out in the end," she said, her voice trailing off.

"Any relationships?" I asked.

"I have drifted in and out of a few. I think my independent streak is the opposite of what most Italian men are looking for. But I, too, ended a relationship awhile ago. It just wasn't very healthy. It hasn't been as smooth of a split as I was hoping it would be," she said quietly.

The wooden planks of the pier moaned under the weight of each step we took. A lone fisherman sat at the end of the pier, casting his line out with the snap of his wrist, flipping his rod and bait, and then sitting patiently waiting for a bite. I stopped and moved toward the edge of the wooden railing, leaning my weight on my forearms, peering off back toward the shore, admiring Bognor from a distance. I picked up my camera bag, took a photo of the lone fisherman and then more of the Bognor coast, and of course Gabriela; she was a natural. The breeze shifted her long hair and her shy beautiful smile made her a very cooperative subject.

"Have you ever modeled?" I asked.

"No," she responded.

"But you've been asked," I continued.

"Yes." Gabriela leaned back with her back and elbows resting against the pier, with me standing directly across from her shooting picture after picture.

"Enough already!" she said, throwing her hands up toward her face.

"OK, OK," I said, bending over to put the camera back in the bag, then standing up opposite of her position again. "Do you know how beautiful you are?"

Gabriela walked the few steps toward me, leaned her body into mine and kissed me. It was a perfect first kiss. At least, that is what I thought. Our lips met and remained together for a couple of seconds, and then Gabriela moved her head back and where our lips left off, our eyes continued. Her brown eyes mesmerized me; nothing was said. The occasional sound of the pier flags rippled softly in the wind, and then I moved back toward her, standing upright, scooping her neck with my fingers and pulling myself back toward her lips. I kissed her gently at first and could feel how well our bodies felt together, fitting together like a glove. Gabriela moved her fingers around to my back, running them up my skin and feeling the muscles around my spine. Gabriela then moved her head, laying it against my shoulder and chest, and I allowed my weight to shift back toward the pier's edge and wrapped my arms around her upper body as she clung to my waist and lower back with her arms, in complete silence. If there was ever a perfect picture for a Valentine's Day card, this was it.

"Should we go?" I asked.

"In a moment. Dum spiro spero," Gabriela whispered.

"What is that?" I replied.

"Oh, just something I heard once," she answered back.

The walk from the pier seemed to be over in an instant. Gabriela slowed, pulling me to the edge before the last few steps would lead us off the pier. She looked back toward the lone fisherman.

"Can you take a picture of that for me?" she asked.

"Of course I can," I replied.

Gabriela looked out from the pier, leaning toward the Bognor coast, and I moved behind her taking her hands in mine. She brought her arms up, wrapping both hers and mine around her shoulders. I moved my face toward Gabriela's face, kissing her lightly on the cheek, then again on the neck.

"Your lips are so soft," she responded.

"You are amazing. Are you ready to go?" I added.

"Where are we going?" Gabriela asked.

"To Salisbury. I've heard they have some amazing Roman structures there. It isn't too far away," I replied, walking her away from the pier.

"Sounds lovely," she replied.

Chapter 14

The summer sun filled our car's interior, spilling in from the sunroof. My hands fumbled with the air conditioning controls on the steering wheel face, at first blasting the cabin with a rush of arctic air. The controls quickly turned down and adjusted to a low, steady stream of cool air. I glanced over at Gabriela, who had fallen asleep. Gabriela's seat was reclined slightly as she slept, with her right foot pulled up and tucked inside the back of her left knee.

I played with the radio, trying to find some music with a familiarity to it. The radio scanned from station to station, stopping for five seconds on each channel playing the Kinks, AC/DC, BBC News, some 80s punk bank that I had always referred to generally as playing "Molly Ringwald music," Adele, The Rolling Stones, Adele again and then finally the tuner rested on Ralph Vaughan Williams, "The Lark Ascending." It seemed fitting as I drove through England that I would listen to Williams, who had become one of my favorite composers, and England's greatest.

My youth had been spent exploring all kinds of musical genres, from pop and rock-and-roll, metal, rap and blues, enjoying at least parts of all of them. My love for classical had developed after college.

My eyes scanned the English countryside, seeing a postcard moment, it seemed, almost every two or three minutes, with the photographer in me wanting to stop and capture every single image. It would be impossible. The highway between Bognor and Salisbury was a four-lane freeway, but I had chosen to work our way more slowly, taking a more scenic route via the much smaller, less traveled back roads. Time was not of the essence.

We passed old homes built centuries before, still considered "newer" by some local standards. The countryside seems to be God's own jigsaw puzzle if viewed from above, with varying shades of green puzzle pieces divided by stone fences thrown up hundreds of years before.

A large flock of sheep came into my view along the left side of the road, dotting the landscape like small white polka dots on a green fabric. I slowed the car, noticing that there was no one behind me or coming up in front of me in the other lane, and I looked for a spot along the road that could serve as a pullout. A small dirt road came into view to my left, adjacent to the field of sheep. The car turned left, pulling off the road down the single land trail that cut between two stone walls, serving as a buffer between two opposite fields, one holding a large flock of my found sheep and the other containing a few cows that were all resting along the far side of the pasture.

I parked the car fifty feet off the highway, not noticing any No Trespassing signs. *Maybe that is an American thing*, I thought. The car was left running, as I didn't want to wake Gabriela. I reached into the backseat and found my camera bag. I stood outside the car, changed the lens and started walking down the dirt road; my subjects awaited me. Summer flowers of varying colors and varieties lined the seldom-used road, beautifying this place regardless of whether they were full-bloom summer flowers or some form of weed. I did not know and actually did not care; they made a great photo.

I squatted on the road, getting as close to ground level as possible without lying in the dirt, and took pictures of this single dirt land road enclosed by two stone walls, thinking about how great this picture would look framed, hanging on the distressed red brick wall in my studio back in Boston.

The sound of talking sheep getting closer focused my attention toward the wall to my right. The pasture dividing wall stood approximately four feet high, extended now even higher with the addition of the heads and hooves of fifteen to eighteen sheep gazing over the fence at their new neighbor.

This image reminded me of a candy shop, and what a line of five-year-old children barely able to peek their noses over the glass counter would look like, with their fingertips seeming to be the only thing keeping them in place. I backed up to the far fence to get as many sheep in this classic picture as possible. Twelve sheep would have to do. No one would believe this was a natural un-edited shot. I shot picture after picture, capturing various poses of "bahhing" and grass chewing, the sheep looking as if a conversation was taking place among them over the latest debates in Parliament.

I wished that I could have gotten a photo of the same scene from the backside, making a pair of photographs that I was sure would win an award in every county fair from Washington State to the Deep South. A National Geographic entry would be a perfect alternative. I moved closer in on a white-faced and black-faced pair that stood side by side, capturing shots of the two of them looking at me as if thinking, "What are you looking at?" Another of them seemed to yell, "Get away from us!" And then finally the sheep looked at each other, giving me the perfect shot.

I went closer, scratching the sheep between their eyes and down their noses, their long tongues reaching up to lick my hand.

"Farewell, my friends," I said with a horrible English accent, laughing to myself.   I turned back toward the car to see that Gabriela was walking toward me.

"Hey," I said. "Did you sleep well? Come over here, I want to introduce you to a few of my new friends." Gabriela laughed.

"Did I just hear you talking to them with a British accent?" she asked.

"A very bad one, but yes you did," I said smiling.

"What am I going to do with you?" Gabriela asked leaning into my shoulder.

The sheep, sensing the attention they had just moments ago dwindling away, began to "bah, bah" loudly.

"I think that it is time to move on," I announced, and we walked back toward the car and I opened Gabriela's door.

"You are such a gentlemen," she remarked.

"I try," I replied.

"Can I see?" Gabriela asked.

"The pictures?" I replied.

She nodded.

"Sure," I said, handing her the camera and showing her how to scroll through all the pictures taken, including the ones of Gabriela on the pier from earlier in the day.

We drove quietly with the radio playing in the background Gustav Mahler's *Symphony #1*, third movement. Before getting back on the road, I had decided to hook up my MP3 player through the car's stereo system. I had a bad habit of channel surfing whenever there was a song on the radio that I didn't like. This way I could just let "my" music play. If Gabriela didn't like it, I told her to change it.

"I was watching you take pictures," Gabriela said while looking through the camera. "Are you always so delicate?"

"Delicate? I'm not sure what you mean," I said. "Do I look feminine?"

"No, silly. I have been watching you. It's not even how kind and considerate you have been to me, but it is just watching you take pictures, of me, on the pier, of those sheep and the scenery back there. You seem to use your camera to gently hold each of your subjects with a tenderness that you would see as a newborn baby is being held in its mother's arms."

This wasn't the first time that I had heard this. In fact, I had thought about this a lot over the past number of years. There was an occasion a year or so after my divorce when Judith, a friend of mine, just completing a degree in counseling, mentioned that she thought that my loveless marriage had created this in me. She had called it, in relationship terms, an "anxious personality," one who over-loves, loves too much with a fear of not being loved in return. Judith believed that my love and care came through in everything else that I did.

I looked over at Gabriela, smiled, reached over and squeezed her hand with a gentle caress. "Thank you. That means a lot to me. I do think that I put my all into everything that I do." Gabriela set the camera in her lap.

"So tell me, what do you know about Salisbury?" I asked.

The sound of conquering trumpets erupted from somewhere in the backseat.

"What was that?" I asked in a state of startledness.

"I'm sorry," Gabriela responded as she twisted her body around to retrieve her bag from the backseat. "It's just my phone. I thought I had turned it down after we left this morning." Gabriela sat back in her seat shifting her back toward the door, seated almost facing me. Her eyes opened wide and her hand had risen to her mouth. "Oh, no. Che cosa sta facendo?"

I asked, "Is everything OK?"

Gabriela exhaled sharply, scrolling her finger up her phone's touch screen. "I can't believe this!" she continued. "I don't know that happened. I have fifty-seven new text messages since we left Bognor. The only thing I can imagine is that my phone rebooted and the volume reverted back to a default setting."

The phone speaker blared again, with the sounds of triumphant trumpets ringing through the car's interior; Gabriela fumbled to turn the volume down. A long pause filled the car, with the faint sounds of Mahler filling the empty silence with a faint sound of echoing timpani.

"It's Marco," Gabriela said with a concerning whisper to her voice. "He has been texting me constantly since we left Bognor."

Another trumpet sound quietly rang from her phone again. "He is upset with me. I guess I should tell you this now. We broke up about a month ago. More correctly, I broke up with him. He hasn't taken it so well."

Gabriela went on to describe their six month relationship. How she and Marco had met at an educational summit in Naples and how aggressively he had pursued her. Gabriela had loved the attention at first. Marco had charmed her and made her feel like a woman and not an object of desire. The distance was also a factor. She had time to breathe. Marco worked for an antiquities firm out of Naples. With both of them working and traveling, they only saw each other on some long weekends. Gabriela had started to see cracks in the romantic facade, the "goodnight" calls turning into "Who were you with today?" calls. The daily flirting texts turned into "Why haven't you responded yet?" texts.

Then just over a month before, Marco had shown up unannounced; a romantic surprise, he had suggested. But after their first night together, Gabriela found Marco looking into her closets, checking out her drawers. He had told her that he was just trying to figure out what it was that she liked to wear; he wanted to surprise her with a gift.

The week with Marco had continued, with Gabriela needing to go to work and leaving him behind unwatched. He told her that he had meetings to go to, contacts to visit, but there was something about leaving him alone in her apartment that unnerved her.

Gabriela came home noticing that her things were out of place. Her dresser drawers were disheveled, and her mail had been opened. Marco arrived back a half hour later, and Gabriela questioned him about why he opened her mail, including her Visa bill.

"I just wanted to see if you needed any help paying your bill!" Marco inserted.

"It is none of your business who I owe money to or how much I owe!" Gabriela had yelled back.

"So who did you stay with in Majorca?" Marco questioned her harshly, pointing at the Visa statement.

"What?" Gabriela had said. "Are you joking with me? I was at a conference."

With that, Gabriela asked him to leave. Marco pleaded and pleaded, but she would not be detoured. She gave him time to pack up his clothing, Marco begging with her the entire time, and then he was gone. Until now.

He had texted off and on since he left, offering words of repentance, seeking atonement from Gabriela.

Gabriela's phone texted again.

"What is he saying to you?" I asked.

"He's been following me," Gabriela responded. "It's like he has been watching me, watching us. I hadn't received anything from him at all for the past week or more, but in all of these texts, fifty-five in just the last couple of hours, he has described where I've been, what I've done. He even described you."

I looked at her. "Do you have a picture of him?"

Gabriela scrolled through her phone looking for a picture of the two of them.

"Here, this is one of the two of us a couple months ago. He hated it when I wore heels out," she remarked.

The picture Gabriela produced for me showed her and Marco standing on the red carpet in front of a museum grand opening in Naples. With her heels on Gabriela seemed to tower over his five-foot-eight-inch frame. I thought that he looked like the stereotypical Italian male as I glanced between the photo and the road, with his slicked back dark hair and opened purple silk shirt. *Only missing a couple layers of gold chains around his neck*, I thought.

"Let me read this text to you," Gabriela said, sifting through the messages. "Here it is. 'You exchanged me for that museum guy in Bognor?'"

"He's been following us?" I asked.

I immediately checked the rearview mirror to see if anyone was following us. It seemed clear, and nothing looked to familiar. I had an idea.

"If he was in Bognor watching us, then there is a good chance that he's following us still," I said, picking up the speed in the car. "Let's see if we can expose him a little bit if he is out here somewhere. Do you think he is dangerous?"

Gabriela gasped, thinking for a moment. "My tires. Yesterday at the bathhouses. Do you think he could do something like that?"

"He's your ex-boyfriend, not mine. You tell me," I replied.

Gabriela answered, "I don't think that I ever felt like I was in harms way with him, but I am now remembering that look in his eyes when he left my apartment. I am not sure anymore."

"What about your tires? Anything that would make you believe he would become violent?" I asked.

"I don't know," Gabriela answered quietly.

A small fruit and vegetable stand appeared and I pulled off the road, checking my rearview mirror; again, nothing. I pulled out my camera, replacing the lens with the most high-speed lens that I brought on the trip.

The fruit stand seemed to be supported by mostly local consumers. There was fresh milk, local vegetables, and fruits arranged in baskets and boxes. I sat down on an empty fruit crate that I moved, giving me a great view of the highway we had just traveled down.

"You're taking pictures?" Gabriela asked.

"Just trust me. These could be the best pictures yet," I replied. "Do they have any oranges?"

I spent about ten minutes snapping picture after picture, looking at my images from time to time. Gabriela found a refrigerated area and a bottle of some kind of green tea energy drink, a couple avocados, and a bag of fresh oranges from Spain.

"Are you ready there, Mr. Photographer?" she asked.

I answered, "I do believe that I am."

Seated in the car, I pulled my camera bag out of the backseat and connected the cables to the laptop that I rested between Gabriela and I. The photo viewer window opened and I selected a picture, bringing it to full screen. Pictures of car after car came into view on the screen, finally stopping on an image of a silver mini-cooper.

"Please tell me no," Gabriela said with a tone of concern.

"I'm afraid the answer is yes," I replied.

As I zoomed in on the driver's side window, the image of Marco came into focus, seemingly looking directly at me in the picture.

"I can't believe that he is here. That he is following me. How would he even be able to?" Gabriela asked.

"Did you have any of this trip planned when he was with you in Rome?" I asked.

"Yes," she answered.

"Did he have access to your itinerary?" I asked.

Gabriela's body froze in thought. Her mind raced at the speed of light, re-living her last week with Marco. Her mind retraced her steps with her plans, and she remembered the emails she had received from the travel service with her flight and reservations for both her car and the two nights at Battle Bed and Breakfast. But she didn't have anything listed at Bognor. If Marco had hacked into her Google account, he would be able to track any of her reservations, but if he had used her laptop while she was working, he would have had access to all of her notes about her trip.

"He could know some basics," she responded. "What if I just fly home? I feel as though I have dragged you into my mess."

"I am not leaving you alone to deal with this psycho guy," I said with a chuckle. "Besides, we have some work to finish." My hand rose from the camera bag and placed the medallion on Gabriela's lap.

Chapter 15

1335 AD

Elizabeth's small hands pushed the wrought iron gate open, causing it to groan in its joints. The gate closed behind her with a click of the hinge and she was safe again. Safety comes in many variations to many individuals, and Elizabeth's safety was located in her rose garden, closing the gate of her outside world and distractions, opening her mind to thinking and creativity.

She had spent the past eight years planning, organizing, planting and now cultivating the Clare roses. Her roses came from the best gardens in Europe, and she took the time to care and nurture each of them individually.

The garden was built on two acres, with an eight foot high red brick wall that served as a defense from the outside world. Wrought iron windows spaced every ten feet around the enclosure allowed for the casual visitor to peek in and admire the garden creation that was located next to the abbey of Cambridge. Grassy walkways wove through the beds of roses that formed crescent moon-shaped cutouts, forming an outside ring of white rose beds. Elizabeth had planted variations of pink roses around the outermost edge of her circular design, then with each subsequent circle inside, the rose colors began to fade to white, lighter and lighter until the center circle of flowers grew with the purest color of white imaginable.

Elizabeth opened her rose doors to visitors through the season, once the flowers came into bloom, but only if she was present to serve as host. Today was not one of those days.

Elizabeth tied the skeleton key to the gate, with its satin ribbon, to the waist tie of her dress and walked around the outer perimeter of the roses enjoying the quiet fragrant-filled stroll. To the average visitor in her garden, it was shaped in a circular design, but to Elizabeth, the view of her rose garden from the nearby bell tower was something completely different. Her garden of roses, white in the center, growing out to pink, formed one single rose, whose individual petals were those same crescent shaped beds, all forming a single flower.

Elizabeth walked slowly, stopping occasionally to caress a fully bloomed bud, drawing her face close and intoxicating herself with each unique smell. She wondered if taken into her garden blindfolded she would be able to recognize each plant individually. She knew she could. The experience would be no different from being able to recognize her own children. Elizabeth was twenty-eight years old, mother of seven children, with each child represented by a layer of color in her garden. She looked at the middle display of white flowers and walked to the center point of her garden and sat on a round bench.

Her eyes looked slowly around the perimeter of the garden, pleased with the way her garden had developed, then heavenward gazing at the late morning clouds, their fluffy composition. She looked toward the abbey tower, the spot of her garden inspiration, her hours of contemplating the garden and design there.

A bow holding her blouse together at Elizabeth's neckline was untied with a gentile pull from her delicate fingers, revealing a porcelain color of skin and a pink ribbon tied around her neck. Elizabeth pulled on the ribbon hidden under her clothing, pulling up another key. She lifted it up from around her neck and sat it in her lap, clasping her hands.

A robin flew from the top of the brick wall, resting in the grass ten feet from Elizabeth, hopping gracefully and looking up at her to see if she was watching. Elizabeth watched as the robin began pulling at the worm, then looked around the perimeter again. The robin hopped toward Elizabeth, the worm dangling from its beak, bouncing with each hop of the red-breasted bird. Elizabeth slowly extended her hand toward the robin. The bird turned its head slightly staring back, and then quickly flew off over the wall.

Elizabeth's fingers ran slowly under the lip on the concrete seat, stopping as her finger felt the groove. She slid off the seat, facing the rock-faced pedestal, counted down three rocks, and as she had done many times before, pried the stone loose revealing a lock. The key that had rested in her lap was inserted, turned, and the rock facade door opened. Elizabeth bent down deeper, peering in the dark cavern underneath the circular pedestal, reached in with her right hand and removed a velvet bag about a foot square. Elizabeth quickly took her seat, leaving the hidden compartment ajar. The key was placed to her right, and she placed the dark red bag with a golden colored rope gathered at the top on her lap. Her fingers trembled as she pushed apart the opening to the bag. Her hand felt its way inside, pulling out five individual bags and placing them to her left.

Elizabeth opened each bag; they looked identical to the larger bag they were carried in. The contents of each were placed on the top of their respective bags, then Elizabeth placed her hands deep in a pocket of an underskirt she wore and removed an identical bag that she placed with the five already laying next to her. The new bag was opened, with a singular item inside.

Elizabeth examined each item looking for imperfections and inconsistencies. There were identical, at least as far as Elizabeth could tell. Each medallion was a mirror image of the next, with all six now in her possession.

"They are finished," Elizabeth whispered.

Her fingers gently ran across the face of the most recent addition, admiring the craftsmanship of Henry, the artisan that Elizabeth had hired ten years before to help her design and build her garden of roses, and more importantly, the medallions. In the past ten years, Elizabeth had begun to trust Henry, and with that trust, Elizabeth had approached him a year prior asking for his help. Henry respected Elizabeth for the kind, caring woman she was and respected her desire for privacy in the creation of each of the medallions. As he was instructed, after each medallion was finished, he was to hand deliver it to Elizabeth before starting on the next. And as she instructed, after delivering the sixth medallion to Elizabeth, Henry would return to his shop and destroy everything that went into their creation.

Chapter 16

I set my phone down, disconnecting the call, and took a big breath of oxygen into my lungs and exhaled it slowly.

"There is an Express-Auto in Salisbury, so we can drop this car off and get something that Marco hasn't seen before. I think you should turn off your laptop, and your phone, and take the battery out of it," I said with a voice of command and concern. "Before we do anything else, let's go get something to eat, get a place, regroup and go from there."

"I am sorry," Gabriela said, reaching over holding my hand. I looked toward her with a questioning furrowed brow. "I am sorry that I have put you through all of this commotion."

"Are you kidding me?" I answered with a smile in my voice. "Wasn't it me who drug you into my own treasure chase?"

Salisbury sat comfortably on a hill, the site of the original fort built by the Romans. Its city center sat in its place with the rest of the city sprawling out down the hilly countryside. I pulled into the Express-Auto shop, noticing that there were only six or seven cars to choose from, including two Mini Coopers, a smaller charcoal Honda Civic, and a black Honda Accord. I walked from the office with a new set of keys spinning from my index finger.

"The clerk was excited to have a Jetta on the lot, plus the Accord will save about twenty pounds a day," I said, opening the trunk. "Let me grab our stuff."

As I loaded the car, my phone's email indicator rang three times. With a quick glance I mumbled to myself, "It's about time."

"Anything important?" Gabriela asked.

"I sent a message to a friend at Boston U about the medallion earlier. He is just getting back to me."

The few pieces of luggage were placed in the trunk compartment; Gabriela was seated on the passenger's side and I sat back in the driver's seat, having to adjust it back as far as it would slide. The fabric seat covers were nothing like the leather seats of the Jetta.

I heard a quiet whisper as I latched my seatbelt into place, and I looked over at Gabriela as she gently ran the beads of her rosary through her fingers. The proper thing to do was to wait until she was done, I thought. My eyes glanced across the street at the smaller shops that lined it.

The scene looked like Harry Potter and Ames, Iowa, had given birth, with what seemed to be mom-and-pop shops, including Elizabeth's Seconds, a secondhand clothing store, Salisbury Antiques, Yellow Submarine Fish Aquariums, and then a McDonald's at the corner of the block. My eyes focused on the red structure located on the opposite sidewalk nearest me. It was the quintessential red British phone booth. *I've got to get a picture of that*, I thought. Gabriela was still deep in prayer so I slid out of the car, camera in hand, and walked toward the street.

The rosary was still swaying from the rearview mirror when I rejoined Gabriela. "Get some good pictures?" she asked.

"You know what? I think I did. What about you? Did you get done what you intended?" I asked.

Gabriela leaned forward kissing the crucifix. "I did. St. Christopher will be here to help protect us."

"I almost forgot about the email," I said, picking the phone out of my pocket. The Gmail icon was selected and I double-clicked on the waiting message from Dr. Russell Bowles. And I read:

Jonah,

Hope you are having a great trip. I did a quick search of the information that you provided. Based on the text, workmanship, and overall look of the medallion, our best guess is it's something made before 1400. I did find a photo of another sample in a university share program that seems to be a match. But I cannot give you any additional information. Sorry. If I find something else out, I will let you know.

Regards,

R. Bowles

"I thought you said you didn't take a picture of it?" Gabriela questioned.

"I didn't with my camera, but I did with my phone. I emailed it to myself, and then deleted it from my phone...Just in case," I responded.

We pulled out of the Express-Auto parking lot, driving toward a deli that was recommended by the car rental staff.

I took a bite of my turkey sourdough; the Swiss cheese seemed much sharper, creating an additional mouth-watering reaction. Gabriela sat down from using the ladies' room. I thought about the scene in the car, the rosary, and Marco. Was there something Gabriela wasn't telling me? Was there more to Marco than she had let on? Was she familiar enough with his anger, enough that it would cause her to bless our car? And then it flashed through my mind. Was it possible that Marco had been following me from the previous morning from the Colchesters' at Battle, shortly after having just met Gabriela? Marco was a dealer in antiquities. What if he had followed me to Battle? What cars were in the parking lot when I left? Do any of them match up with the car Marco was driving a couple hours before?

Afternoon clouds began to gather with an ominous black presence growing from the southern coast that moved toward Salisbury. A wind grew in strength, quickly filling the north/south streets like an invisible tsunami carrying any street debris with it. Paper wrappers from discarded McDonald's hamburgers swirled in the corners of adjacent buildings, floating up and down with the current of each breath of wind.

Gabriela and I finished our lunch and walked out as the first drops of rain started down, slowly at first like the beating of a single drum keeping beat to a march, and then the drumming multiplied to a stadium full of snare drums beating faster and faster, beating on the roof of our car. The rain came down hard.

"Where did that come from?" I asked, wiping off the excess water from my head and shoulders. "I mean, storms can come out of nowhere in Boston, but that was ridiculous."

"This is England, Jonah. It rains like this all the time," Gabriela said with the voice of a middle school teacher.

The email indicator on my phone rang again. I retrieved it, seeing that there was another message from my friend Dr. Bowles.

"Now let's see what Dr. Bowles has for us this time," I said.

The only information included in the email was a link to a Web site and a brief message: "Having fun?" The link brought up a news site, bbc.co.uk, with a video posting for a story labeled "The Conqueror Vandalized?" It began:

"For almost a thousand years a memorial has stood at the spot of one of the most significant places in English history. The Battle Mount marks the location of the death of King Harold and the conquering of King William in 1066. Park officials say that within the past forty-eight hours, someone, or something, came here to this wall and attempted to topple this ancient structure. Although there are no signs of using of any explosives or outside tools, park officials claim that someone forced one of the stones of this wall out of place, and then tried to glue it back together again. The stone in question, seen here, seems to have been hollowed out, whether from the culprit or someone ages ago, then reattached and put back into place. A park volunteer of the past sixteen years, making her rounds like she does every evening, noticed the stone's misplacement almost immediately."

"I was looking around the grounds looking for anyone with any questions or needing any help. I saw the stone sticking out immediately."

"Maude Chatsworth called the parks office immediately and officials were out this morning examining the stone, discovering the hollowed-out center. Whoever is at fault here couldn't seem to put ole

Humpty Dumpty back together again. If you have any information, please call the local metro police at 1.983.403.0292.9. Jennifer Shumway, BBC news, Battle.

"So what are you thinking now?" Gabriela asked. "Are you concerned at all?"

"Of course I am concerned, but for maybe a lot of different reasons. I think that by turning this medallion in now…" I paused. "We need to solve this mystery. Too many questions are out there without any answers. Plus there's you, Marco, and your safety. I am not risking a distraction that could put you in harm's way."

Something told me that my trip could last longer than I had anticipated, and if Marco had us under surveillance at each of the previous nights' bed-and-breakfasts', it might make it easier for him to track us down. A little more privacy wouldn't hurt either.

"Good evening. I am Ana, Welcome to the Salisbury Hilton. What can we help you with?" came the mousy little voice from a mousy little woman in her mid-twenties standing behind the motel's front desk.

"We would like a room for a couple of nights," I answered.

"One or two beds?" Ana asked.

"Do you have a room with a soaking tub and a queen bed?" Gabriela asked.

"Let me check." Ana tapped a few strokes on the computer.

I looked around the lobby, noticing that it didn't look much different from any other hotel I had stayed at in the States. The smell was the most familiar scent, and I wondered if there was a company somewhere that manufactured industry aromas; sprays so that all hotels, all high schools, and all grandparents' houses smelled the same within their category. Two nights of grandma-smell in the bed-and-breakfasts was enough; hotel-smell would work just fine for a couple days.

"I have a couple rooms available that fit your criteria," Ana announced. "We have a single room with a soaking tub or a room with a kitchenette and tub. The kitchenette includes a sink, toaster, microwave, and a hot plate. There are some pots and pans as well as individual spice and oil packets."

I looked confused. "Think of them like ketchup packets, only with oil, dried basil, or peppers. Stuff like that," Ana replied.

"We'll take the kitchenette room," I answered. "Is there any place to buy some groceries nearby?"

"A couple blocks away, around the corner from the Bank of England," Ana replied, pointing out toward the direction needed to go to get there.

"Thank you," I answered, then signed a copy of the credit card receipt.

"I'll send a porter out to bring your stuff to your room. You will be in room 1903," she added.

"1903?" Gabriela asked. "This hotel isn't that tall!"

"We get that question all the time," Ana answered. "When the hotel was originally built in the 1980s, they were going to build it twenty stories tall, but the city council rejected it because of the massive size. Plans were changed and the motel was cut down to only five stories. The owner decided to keep the numbering from the original top five stories. The bottom floor is the sixteenth floor."

"Interesting," Gabriela replied.

"I'll bring the car up to drop off our luggage," I said. "Then we can go grab a couple things from the market."

Ana had provided a loaner umbrella from the hotel and Gabriela and I walked back to our car in search of Currell's Market, the grocer that Ana had recommended. The rain continued to pour down on the coast, with the windshield wipers working overtime to keep a clear view out the front window. I turned back toward the direction of the Express-Auto shop.

"Where are we going?" Gabriela asked. "I thought the clerk told us to go in that direction," pointing her finger across my line of view.

"Can we make a quick detour?" I asked.

"Sure," she answered.

"I'm sorry. I should have asked you before I decided for the both of us," I responded back.

Our Accord led us into a small parking lot across the street from the car rental office and Gabriela asked, "Are you taking me to McDonald's?" in a flirty sarcastic voice.

I laughed. "Not even close. Can we run into an antique store real quick?"

"Sure," Gabriela answered. "Can I warn you that some of the stuff in the stores are not antiques at all? Maybe more like antiqued. This is a tourism city, you know."

I smiled. "I know. I just wanted to look around for a bit."

The Salisbury Antique Store entry opened with a bell ringing above the door. The store was decorated from top to bottom with every form of decor imaginable. I thought back to the Colchesters' hallway and its potpourri of wall hangings and photos—this place was that on steroids. The smell of mothballs and mold/mildew was overwhelming; especially in a building that Gabriela thought was about three hundred years old.

An older man of about seventy rose from a desk located in the back of the shop and began inching his way toward us. I thought he was about five feet nine inches, but his frail body bent in his shoulders, making him much shorter. His head was bald, with the exception of a grayed ring of growth that circled his head stopping just above his ears, and his nose protruded out with a pair of reading glasses clinging to his flared nostrils, stopping them from sliding off completely.

"Evening, folks. Welcome to Salisbury Antiques," he said in a Scrooge-like voice. "Anything I can help you with?"

"We are in the city for a couple of days and thought we would stop in and take a look at your shop," Gabriela answered.

"Well, we do have a few items from your occupation," he said.

"My occupation?" she replied. *How does he know what my occupation is?* she thought.

"The Romans, aren't you from Italy?" he said with a thick accent. "You occupied England for a thousand years."

"Yes, I am," she answered back.

"My dear, I can spot an accent a hundred kilometers away. Seems all we do business with anymore are foreigners. I'm afraid before too long we'll have sold our entire country away."

"Do you have anything that you specialize in?" I asked.

"Oh, a Yankee! Sounds like a faint New England dialect I hear there," he replied.

I laughed. "Very good. I've been in Boston for the past ten years. I guess I've picked it up more than I imagined."

"Please allow me to introduce myself. My name is Alistair Throckmorton," he said, extending his hand. Gabriela took his hand first and then I did, both noticing how large his hands were for a "shorter" man. I felt the thinness of his long fingers, creating a looseness of his skin, and his immaculately manicured nails. "Owner-operator," he added.

"Jonah," I said...then cut myself off. *No names, no names*, I thought. *Marco is out there somewhere.*

"Well, I'll let you two look around. I'll be back here if you have any questions," Alistair said, turning around and pulling up the sleeves of his light blue-gray cardigan sweater, which had fallen down covering most of his hands and seemed to be a couple sizes too large to begin with. I watched him slowly walk back toward his desk, using a trail between the various furniture pieces to support himself with each stop. *I do not want to get old*, I thought.

Gabriela had begun looking at the various furniture pieces that were on display. Elizabethan rocking chairs, Victorian dressers, Hanover benches, and then she found a guidebook of Salisbury and its Roman origins. "Perfect," she whispered.

I made my way through the maze of wooden household designs, knowing that I wouldn't be purchasing anything to ship home, unless an amazing deal was found. "Mr. Throckmorton, do you have any paper products? Deeds, stock certificates, books, signatures?" I asked.

"If you look over by the wall, next to those wooden globes, that is where most of the scriptopoly will be found," he replied.

My eye caught something that I couldn't believe. "What can you tell me about this wooden globe?" I asked.

Alistair started. "It is a solid sphere of oak. It measures 40.5 inches around the equator and is a masterful example of relief art." The artist had carved down any area of water around the earth. "Based upon the land masses depicted, it dates around 1800. It is all original with the exception of the metal spindle that it turns on."

I looked at the gorgeous workmanship of the globe. I picked it up feeling its weight and noticed that, with the exception of a few cracks in the wood around the North Pole, it was in amazing condition. Santa should be careful. The price tag of eight hundred pounds, or sixteen hundred US dollars, was a bit out of my price range. Or was it?

I found a book of paper products that I started to flip through the pages of. Each document was protected by a plastic page protector, and included a brief history and description of the item. There were canceled checks written by Elton John as payment to a construction company, price of seventy five pounds, a land bill of sale from 1833, a signed black-and-white photo of Charlie Chaplin, and then I saw it, and I knew it in an instant.

It reminded me of that Christmas ten years before, and my last minute rush to go buy my ex-wife's Christmas gifts. My arms had been filled with various odds and ends of gift possibilities, until I walked around the aisle and I saw a cashmere sweater. It was perfect. Immediately I knew everything in my arms did not even compare.

There I stood looking at a stock certificate dated January 24, 1923, for the Joplin Photography Company. It was perfect, perfect for my studio. It depicted a Greek goddess model that was not unusual on stock certificates during that time period, only she was taking a photograph with a Joplin camera, with the ink in a faint rose red. The price tag: fifty pounds, or one hundred dollars. Perfect.

"Do you have any questions for me?" Mr. Throckmorton's voice called out from his desk.

"I think I found something," I said. "Me too," Gabriela echoed.

"Really, what did you find?" I added.

Gabriela held up a framed black-and-white photograph, measuring about fifty by twenty-four inches, of Salisbury from the turn of the last century, showing details of the original wall from the Roman times surrounding the city.

"How much is it?" I asked.

"Only forty pounds," Gabriela answered.

We spent another half hour perusing through the shop, feeling a bit like we were the subjects of a reality TV show; our own version of *American Pickers*. I picked up a book, *The Legends of Britannia*, copyright 1931, and I still really wanted the wooden globe. Gabriela was content with her photograph, although there was an original oil painting from a local artist, Jane Smythe, of the countryside with dots of white sheep in the distance; it reminded her of home, and it reminded her of the sheep earlier in the day. She didn't know how to get it home.

"Should we go?" Gabriela asked. "I think that Mr. Alistair is getting ready to leave."

I looked over as Mr. Throckmorton was moving sweaters and scarfs around his coat rack uncovering his raincoat.

"I think we are ready to go here," I said.

"Lovely. The cash register is right up front there," Alistair said, pointing to the desk near the front window looking out over the street.

I handed Gabriela the keys. "Do you want to go warm up the car?"

"Sure, but I need to pay for my photograph," she replied.

"Tell you what. I will pay for this and you can buy the food," I said.

Gabriela smiled. "Deal!"

Mr. Throckmorton and I finished the transaction. "I'll see you tomorrow," I said, hearing the door bell ring. Gabriela stood as if the ghost of Julius Caesar himself were looking at her. She silently mouthed something to me.

"What?" I whispered. She mouthed again, with me still not understanding. I said, "Let's go. I think you are hungry."

"Marco is out there!" she finally whispered, pointing to the Express-Auto lot across the street.

I looked out the window, seeing Marco peering into the windows of the Jetta that we had left there earlier. "Honey, do you have our umbrella?" I asked winking at Gabriela. "The last thing we want is for your photograph to get wet."

"It's right here, sweetheart," she replied.

Gabriela and I thanked Alistair and slowly opened the door and the umbrella in unison. "You know its bad luck to open that indoors, don't you?" Mr. Throckmorton announced.

"I think we'll take our chances," I replied, smiling back at him.

Gabriela and I stood close to each other under the black rain protector. Marco had walked toward the front of the rental office that had already closed. We quickened our pace toward the waiting car, looking back to see if Marco had seen us. There was no sign of him. The doors to the Accord were unlocked, allowing Gabriela to get inside quickly. I loaded the antiques in the hatch and joined her in the front seat.

"Well, he either was tracking the car or your phone. He doesn't know where we are," I said.

"Let's hope so," Gabriela whispered.

I pulled the car out of the parking lot, passing the antique store. The Open sign turned off, and Alistair Throckmorton opened the door, waving as we passed. Across the street, Marco was pounding on the door to the rental shop. I looked at my watch— 6:20 pm.

"Just in time," I said. "He can't talk to anyone tonight."

"But what about tomorrow?" Gabriela replied, shifting her body down in her seat. "We will deal with that in the morning. Tonight, you are OK."

And with that, Gabriela and I drove in silence, with the sound of windshield wipers pulsing back and forth, interrupted only by the staccato beating of raindrops against the car's exterior.

The parking brake was pulled, the ignition was turned off and I looked over at Gabriela's worried expression.

"Are you ready?" I asked, grabbing the latch to my door.

"I don't know. I am nervous," she answered.

"Don't be." I leaned over toward Gabriela, kissing her on the cheek. She turned, facing me, and then kissed me lightly on the lips.

"Let's go get some food," Gabriela said.

"Currell's Market awaits." And I opened the door.

Chapter 17

The sound of the door locking into place behind her was the sound of relief and safety for Gabriela; the hotel room was out of Marco's reach, and served as her very own motte and bailey. She had been on the edge from first noticing Marco's texts at the sheep pasture, but those nerves had escalated from the moment she had spotted Marco across the street from Alistair's antique shop.

I turned down the shortened hall to our right, finding the small kitchenette tucked away before the bathroom.

"Are you hungry?" I asked. There was no answer. The large paper grocery bag filled with a few selected items from Currell's Market was set down, and I called out again. "Hey, are you OK in there? You haven't fallen asleep already, have you?"

Still nothing. I peeked my head around the corner to the main area of the room. Gabriela stood quietly at the window staring out over the rain-soaked parking lot and beyond.

I walked up caressing her shoulders with my hands, causing her to jump, startled, as though she had drifted off to another place. She had.

"Hey, are you OK?" I whispered.

Gabriela turned quickly, burying her head into my chest, wrapping her arms around my torso. I understood at this point what Gabriela needed was to be held. She needed the safety that this room and my arms could provide. Nothing needed to be said, nothing could be fixed at this point, only an embrace of reassurance, so I offered that to her. Then it started, slowly at first, and growing with each second the waves of tears started to flow from her soul. From the deepest parts of her body came wave after wave of pain, consuming her body with tremors and aftershocks. The rains continued, both outside on the southern coast of England and down the front of my shirt.

I finally broke the silence. "Are you going to be all right?" I asked, rubbing my fingertips up and down her spine. She nodded her head, still pressed against my chest. "Can I get you a tissue?" Gabriela nodded again. A box of tissues sat on the nightstand next to the bed. I released my clutch of Gabriela and helped her wipe away the effects of the day and the past six months.

I thought for a moment. "I have a great idea."

"Hmmm," was the only response Gabriela could muster.

"How about I go start you a bath, then you can go relax for a bit while I make us something for dinner?" I asked.

"I've never had a man do that for me before," she said.

"Make you a bath?" I asked laughing.

"No, silly man, make me dinner," Gabriela responded, wiping away the last of her tears.

"Well, I am not promising anything. I do know that I feel a bit uncomfortable making pasta for an Italian, that's for sure," I said, picking up the TV remote and finding something to give our room some additional noise.

"I am sure that it will taste wonderful," she said.

"Even if it is a bit Americanized?" I asked.

"Even better," Gabriela said, touching her hand softly against my chest. "Lei e un uomo dolce dolce."

"I love it when you talk to me like that," I responded.

"I will go start my own bath," Gabriela stated, and then retrieved a bag from her luggage filled with various bottles and tubes needed for her bath.

"Take your time," I said. "It could take me a bit to cook."

I walked toward the kitchenette and the bag of groceries that awaited me.

Cooking had become my thing at an early age. My parents had divorced at the beginning of my high school career, and I had stayed with my father. That is when my love affair with cooking had started. I am not sure if it was from my father, or from a "cook or starve" approach, but I had learned.

The garden grown by my father was enormous, lined with rows and rows of every vegetable imaginable. There were tomatoes, green beans, onions, varieties of squash, potatoes, carrots, cucumbers, and eggplants, to name a few. I had spent hours weeding, watering, and harvesting the garden, much to my displeasure at the time.

My father was a cook, a very good cook, but from an old school, or Old Country, perspective; *way too many onions*, I had thought. Everything seemed to be a stew, a casserole, or a crock-pot creation, and in the definition of my father, cooking meant simmering, simmering for hours. Why cook something and have individual flavors when you could cook it all together into one taste?

I was confused when I followed my first recipe in college, finding that something could be prepared and cooked all within the space of thirty minutes. Once I got married the love affair with cooking had come into full blossom, and the flavors started to separate. I cooked dinner after dinner, following recipe after recipe, then learned herb after herb and taste after taste. I hadn't followed a recipe in almost ten years, and my kids had loved my cooking, except for the fact that they thought that I cooked with too many onions.

I set the food on the counter, putting the creams, butters, and cheeses in the fridge and started preparing the pasta and vegetables.

Gabriela cracked the bathroom door, asking me how things were coming along.

"Great!" I replied. The aroma of the products in Gabriela's bath smelled wonderful. *No wonder she smelled so good; she simmers in it*, I thought, laughing to myself. The door closed to the tub room and I began to cook.

I roasted garlic and shrimp, chopped tomatoes, boiled pasta, toasted bread, then mixed onions, basil, olive oil, butter, creams, and the pasta, and dinner was served.

Gabriela called out to me, walking out of the bathroom finding me seated on the bed, picnic-style.

"Are you kidding me?" she asked. The bed was decorated with a blanket that I had pulled from the closet. Two serving platters with stainless steel covers were removed, displaying shrimp scampi, with an appetizer of bruschetta.

Gabriela finished the glass of wine, setting it on the nightstand coaster, and then readjusted the robe still being worn from her bath. "Are you coming back?" she asked.

I appeared from the bathroom, having changed into something a lot more comfortable: a pair of shorts and baggy T-shirt.

"Dishes are done, and I am ready to crash," I announced.

"Dinner was delicious," Gabriela told me. "Where did you come from?"

I laughed, turned on a movie and took my place on the bed next to Gabriela. "Are you comfortable?" I asked as Gabriela nuzzled her entire body against mine.

Her wet, curly, dark brown hair brushed against my cheek, shoulder and arm, smelling like Mother Earth herself with all of the aromas that she provides. Gabriela nodded her head, then wrapped her hand around my chest, clinging to me. I kissed her forehead and rubbed her back.

"He hit me," Gabriela whispered gently. "He told me if I ever left him, I would be sorry."

I lay speechless, wondering what kind of a person, what kind of a man would do anything like that to Gabriela, to any woman for that matter. She was the sweetest, most kind woman. It baffled me. Gabriela went on to tell more of their six-month relationship and how possessive Marco had become, demanding more and more of her time and all of her energy. It was the week that Marco had arrived unannounced. He had become crazed looking around her apartment for a clue of a boyfriend, a past boyfriend, someone that showed interest at all, something or someone that would validate his fears. But he found nothing.

Gabriela told me of Marco's first marriage to Sabine, and the cryptic phone message she had left on Gabriela's phone.

"Beware of the wolf who sharpens his teeth then invites the sheep to dinner," Sabine had said.

Marco had told Gabriela that their divorce was amiable, that he and Sabine had drifted apart in the final couple years of their marriage, but the fear that Gabriela heard in Sabine's voice still was one of terror and anxiety. Marco had opened Gabriela's mail, found the charge at the hotel in Majorca, and the wolf had shown his teeth.

Gabriela had told him not to be silly, that she had been at a conference, and then Marco had backhanded her, spilling her into a glass-top coffee table, leaving her with a cut on her shoulder that required twenty-four stitches, not to mention the bloodied lip and bruise on her cheek.

That had been enough, enough for a woman who had existed on her own being without the support of a man before Marco, and for damn sure didn't need one again. But then there came Jonah, a man whom she had assumed was another typical guy who was only interested in what she could provide naked at a moment's notice. But she was wrong; at least, she wanted to believe that.

She had taken a chance by following her gut when he had invited her to Bognor, and his gentleness had strengthened her feeling. He was the guy she had always wanted in her life, she said. But there was a lot more to learn about him, and the little problem of a certain body of water that lay between them, often referred to as the Atlantic Ocean.

My phone rang. I looked over and picked it up. "I'll be right back," I said and got up and walked toward the bathroom. "Hey sweetheart," I said, and I closed the door.

~

Are you kidding me? Gabriella thought. *I finally tell him about Marco, and I am finding out he has a girlfriend.....a wife? A million scenarios raced through my head, but what was I suppose to do? It's not exactly like I have any control of this situation. No car, I know no one, and if I turn on my phone and/or laptop Marco could find me in an instant.*

~

I opened the bathroom door. "Do you want to say 'hi' to her? OK honey, let me put you on speakerphone." I covered the mouthpiece with my thumb. "Do you mind saying 'hello' to my daughter Lilly?"

Gabriela smiled. "I would love to."

The phone call was disconnected, erasing Lilly's picture from the screen.

"What an adorable girl," Gabriela said, looking at me with a big smile.

"I know. Sorry to run off on you like that. She is working on a project at school that I had forgotten about." I pulled out a ten-inch laminated photograph cutout of Lilly. "It is called 'Where on the Earth?' and each student is given a task of sending these pictures all over the world if possible and have pictures taken of themselves in unique places. She needed a photo to show her class tomorrow, and I remembered it as soon as I saw her name on my caller ID." I took a picture of her with the image of Queen Elizabeth on the wall in the bathroom. "It's a good start. Can you help remind me?" I asked Gabriela.

"Of course I will," she responded. "I am going to go brush my teeth," she said, rummaging through her bag.

"Mmmm, garlic breath. I'll be right behind you," I said, cupping my hand over my nose and mouth.

I switched off the light to the bathroom and walked into the room; Gabriela was waiting for me in bed, pulling up the blanket and sheet and inviting me in next to her. She was wearing a pair of boy shorts and a silk spaghetti-strapped tank, and I, in my shorts and Red Sox T-shirt, slid in next to her. Gabriela immediately slid over my leg, resting her hand on my chest. She sat up and turned off the light next to the bed, leaving a couple of lights through our window off in the Salisbury distance as the only escape from utter darkness. My hands slowly traced the muscles of Gabriela's back, then moved up her vertebrae one at a time.

"We can't do this," I said looking at her, with my eyes now having adjusted to the darkness of the room. She looked at me, kissed me and pulled me toward her.

Gabriela woke up moving her hand across the bed, feeling for the body that had been there and had held her all night, but the bed was cold against her hand and empty. She groaned, stretching her hands above her head. "Miele, dove sei?" she asked in a singing voice.

"Hey beautiful, are you awake? Breakfast is almost ready. Are you ready for my Italian omelet?" I asked from around the corner.

"Come back to bed!" she answered.

I walked around the corner and stood at the foot of the bed, and Gabriela sat up grabbing my hand and pulling me to it. She kissed me passionately. "Come to bed with me for a while," she said.

"We cannot do this for so many reasons," I said.

"Like?" she responded with a devilish smile.

"Well, first of all, you are in no position emotionally to do this. It would be wrong for all the right reasons. My point is that I want to be with you more than anything, but not if it is going to be something I will regret after."

Afterward, I packed the car, pulled it around to the front of the hotel and went up to get Gabriela.

"So what is the plan for the day?" she asked.

"A surprise," I said.

Chapter 18

It was an escape, one that has been felt by many others over the history of time, the ability to finally breathe the air of freedom again, from a jailhouse, a prison, graduation from school, retirement, or a timely divorce; Gabriela was breathing that freedom right now.

Our car sped away through the rain-soaked countryside, leaving behind her own personal purgatory, even through the down pouring of rain; to Gabriela there was nothing but clear skies.

I looked toward her, watching as she sang out loud "Walking on Sunshine" by Katrina and the Waves with the energy of a groupie in the front row of the music festival at Glastonbury.

"You seem to be in a better mood today," I remarked, but was not heard over the sounds vibrating from the speakers. In fact, if I hadn't actually seen the rain I was driving through, I would never have believed it. All I could hear was Gabriela and Katrina singing in unison, not the smacks of the large raindrops on the windshield, not the thumping of the storm on the top of our car, and not the swishing of the wake of water on the freeway surface created by the car's tires pushing away water.

There was so much about Gabriela that I didn't know; so much about me that she didn't know, for that matter. My thoughts circled around questions of, where did this side of her come from?

Is this a mechanism to deal with her stress? Or was it really her reaction to a complete sense of freedom?

I had thought that on this day, getting Gabriela as far away from Salisbury and Marco as possible would be the best thing for her psyche and emotional health. Even though the hotel room was unknown to Marco and it had provided a night of respite, a larger change was necessary. I believed that change should be Stonehenge.

The singing continued as Gabriela found an 80s station, weaving between Queen singing "Bohemian Rhapsody," "Tainted Love" by Soft Cell, and then "Pass the Dutchie" by Musical Youth. I decided to pull into a lone gas station at an intersection, hoping that the change of pace would bring the Italian songbird back to earth.

"I am going to run in and get a drink. Can I get you anything? Do you want to come in?" I asked.

"No, I think I'm going to stretch my legs and get some fresh air. Would you mind getting me water or iced tea or something?" she responded touching my hand.

"Got it," I said, opening my door to a wall of rain water.

"Good morning, laddie. How are we this beautiful mornin'?" said a voice coming from the front of the store. I looked up to find a man who had been pulled directly out of the pages of the "Encyclopedia of Stereotypes," under the heading "Ugly Scotsman."

"Good morning. I guess it could be worse. No one is building an ark. At least, not that I've heard about!" I replied.

A laugh of exaggeration leapt from his large mouth, the home of cricket-yellowed teeth that his lips seemed to have a hard time containing when closed. His thick red hair was unkempt and his sideburns extended down to full chops. Then there was the clothing: a pink polo shirt and a red, green, and black kilt.

"Ah, a Yankee we have here, do we?" He spoke with the thick accent of a Scotsman, but not Sean Connery's, I thought.

"Indeed, indeed," I replied. "Are you just passing through or did ya finally come to yer senses and move back 'ome?" he asked with a chuckle.

"Well, I'm just traveling through, but with all this beautiful weather out, I might not want to go back!" I replied with a smile.

"Are ya needing anything else?" he asked while ringing up our water, teas, and a pack of breath mints.

That'll do, Scotty, that'll do, was all I could think, but my mouth said, "No, thank you. That's everything."

Normally I would have wanted to stay and converse with the kilted Scot, but I wanted to get back to Gabriela, and beside that the guy was kind of creepy. The rain continued to fall down steadily as I walked out and then hurriedly went in the direction of the car parked fifty feet away. I opened the car door to hear the voice of Gabriela fade off into nothing, and then a quick rustle of her bag, which was then thrown to the floor in front of her. I took my place in the seat next to her.

"Were you talking to someone?" I asked, wondering if she had been singing with the radio still.

"No, I'm OK, just thinking out loud," she replied.

The varieties of drinks purchased were picked through as we pulled out of the parking spaces. Gabriela selected a drink and the car was back on the road. Trumpets blared, coming from the bag, from the phone that had been turned on in Gabriela's purse.

The road ahead of us continued to fill with water, although now the sound of each drop hitting the windshield and each wringing of the clouds above dropping moisture on our car seemed to echo louder and louder. Gabriela leaned forward, pulled her phone from her bag and removed the battery. The silence between us intensified as the sounds of Mother Nature continued to use our car as a punching bag.

"I'm sorry," Gabriela said in the whispered tone of a small girl who had just spilled grape juice on her mother's favorite white linen tablecloth.

I knew if anything I couldn't be upset, I couldn't reprimand her. I couldn't scold her, berate her, lecture her or accuse her. That was what she expected me to do. That is what Marco had done and she had lived with those memories.

I had seen the fear in her only when it was safe; only when she felt fortified in our hotel safe haven had she relaxed and then wept. I thought about the emotional barricade she had built up, not showing fear when Marco had begun texting, even when she saw the images of him driving past us in his car. I had seen the crack in her wall at the antique store, the nervous reaction to Marco across the street like the force of an opposing army charging repeatedly at the crack, her wall collapsed and she wept into my shirt for ten minutes.

She expected me to be upset; I reached over and held her hand.

Gabriela had no obligation to me, and I couldn't expect anything from her. I had heard once that expectations are only preconceived disappointments. I had no idea who she was talking to, and I wasn't going to ask.

"So I thought, on this glorious morning we should go to Stonehenge. Have you ever been before?" I asked.

Gabriela paused, almost as if she wanted to confess, tell me the who, what, where, when, and why of her phone call. I gently squeezed her hand, hoping she would understand that it wasn't necessary. She looked at me with tears in her eyes, understanding my gesture.

"I have never been," she answered.

With a gentle tap of her index finger and tissue the water in the corners of her eyes was gone, and out on the plains of Salisbury Stonehenge appeared, and the clouds parted and the rains stopped.

Stonehenge to the first-time visitor is a unique experience, to say the least. It is similar to seeing the Mona Lisa for the first time. The Mona Lisa stares back at you with eyes piercing through your soul, taut lips that speak volumes and an unassuming beauty brought to life by Leonardo da Vinci; so sat Stonehenge, reverently on the Salisbury plain alone. There is no McDonald's next door peddling a happy meal with a Stonehenge replica made of chicken nuggets. There isn't an amusement park across the street called Stonehengeland with a roller coaster named the Stone Age Flyer, that serves forty-four ounce drinks called Druid Fluid, and a kid's plastic crown made to look like the ancient stone calendar/temple/sacrificial altar.

This was something I loved about the English, their overall love and respect of history, and keeping sacred things sacred. The parking lot was nearly empty as we exited our car. The clouds that consumed most of the sky would be a great photo, I thought.

The clouds parted with a column of sunshine pouring down on the stone structure, and I left Gabriela behind to get some shots before the crowds arrived.

"Jonah, come over here," Gabriela called out, motioning to me to join her.

We walked and talked hand in hand about who had built this mammoth structure, and what was its purpose. Gabriela looked in amazement at the architectural feat of moving the massive stones up twenty-four feet, laying them precisely into place.

"Jonah, where is the medallion?" Gabriela asked.

"It's in the bag here," I answered, tapping the bag with the hand that was resting over my shoulder.

"Can I see it?" she asked.

I looked around to see if there was anyone watching us. Was it safe to bring it out in public?

"Just keep it discreet. We really don't need anyone asking any questions," I answered.

"You know I will," she responded.

Then in a mode that I had forgotten about, and hadn't seen since the Battle baths, Gabriela turned into the architecturologist that she was. I followed in tow as she moved slowly around the circular stone structure while clasping the medallion between her hands. She studied each standing stone, each stone lying down, each gap, every gap, and every stone. Her hands rubbed together almost as if trying to release the medallion genie to speak to her; and then she spoke to me. Her eyes widened, and a smile broke across her face, and she became giddy like a sixteen-year-old girl hanging up the phone after receiving an invitation by John Masters, the star quarterback on the high school football team, to be his date for the upcoming homecoming dance.

Gabriela hopped in place, turning slowly toward me with each hop.

"I know! I know! I know!" she repeated.

"You know what?" I answered.

""The medallion...It's Stonehenge!" she cried out, and then tempered her voice so as not to attract attention.

"The medallion is Stonehenge?" I replied.

"The medallion grooves. They are cut in the pattern of the stones and gaps around Stonehenge," she declared.

The next half hour was spent verifying the newly found information. We traced the medallion's shape onto paper, and then found a brochure from the visitor's center with an aerial photograph of the World Heritage site. It matched!

It was now confirmed, at least in our minds—a photographer/history geek from Boston, Massachusetts, and an architect/archeologist from Rome, Italy—the medallion was a clue. From the beginnings it felt like a clue, hidden in a hollowed out stone, Joseph of Arimathea's name scrambled, the X, and now the grooves around the edge.

"What should we do now?" Gabriela asked, as excited as if we had found the city of Atlantis or Bigfoot.

I thought for a moment and said, "Let's go. We are heading to Glastonbury."

Chapter 19

There is a bi-polar personality disorder to Glastonbury, and we felt it from the moment we arrived. On one hand, Glastonbury holds the unique distinction of being the cradle of Christianity in England, the place that legend speaks of as being where Jesus Christ had visited with Joseph of Arimathea, his uncle, while in his twenties. It was also thought to be the place that Joseph came back to after the crucifixion of Christ, and he was believed to have brought with him the Holy Grail, and even the remnants of the thorny bush used for Christ's crown of thorns.

Thousands of visitors make pilgrimages here each year to drink freely from the town's unequaled history and its undeniable spirituality, and to experience the Glastonbury Abbey, its reverent rolling hills and all the sites and signs of those they meet while there.

I likened it to the Loch Ness phenomenon—not whether he/she exists, but in that I am sure if I stood on the shoreline of Ness, each ripple, each wave seen off in the distance would without question seem to be the ancient mariner, Nessy, rising to the surface, calling out to me of his or her existence, without me knowing the water disturbance was actually a combination of reflection and the cresting of the Loch in mid-afternoon breezes; and so was the mystery of Glastonbury. Not verified factually, but the legend and history had created its own reality.

Glastonbury's alter ego was the Glastonbury Music Festival, an annual display of the most popular rock/rap/pop/soul acts in the world. On any given year you could see the likes of U2, AC/DC, Lady Gaga, BB King, the Red Hot Chili Peppers, and dozens of other local and international acts.

These two personalities in my mind seemed to fit together like the Bible being read aloud by Snoop Dogg. Something didn't seem to fit, but maybe a milkshake called a Glastonberry could be purchased during the festival; sacred things remained sacred, at least fifty-one weeks a year.

The cobblestone side streets were beginning to dry from the storm earlier in the day, with moisture remaining only in the seams of the stones. Gabriela and I looked for the Glastonbury Historical Museum located on King Street, just off the main road that divided the city into two halves.

"1114 King Street. It should be the last office down," Gabriela said, passing 1102, Glastonbury Candles.

The address of 1114 appeared at the end of the block, taking up the entire corner of the building. There were six steps leading up to the door and I noticed how the large windows illuminated the museum from both outside walls, letting in as much sun as possible. The wooden floor looked recently refurbished, reflecting a brightness of the sun as we walked in. It was quiet, with the educated silence of a library. A group of nuns seemed to be the main source of visitors, wearing their black robes and habits and white head bands, each with a crucifix that sat protectively against their abdomens, and a pink twisted rope that circled their waists, tied in a loose knot hanging to their knees. They looked up one by one as we entered, smiled gently at us for a moment and then continued to peruse through the museum.

It was a museum, but seemed to be much more than that. The main room held a massive collection of books against most of the two walls that sat opposite the windows, allowing patrons to take the books back to reading tables and spend as much time in review of them as necessary. The center of the room housed a circular information desk with two museum staff members on duty. The first was a sixty-year-old, heavy-set woman whom I noticed had lost most of the hair on the top of her head, with gray/white curls falling down from the sides, almost trying to make up for the top, and horned rimmed reading glasses perched on her nose with a gold chain securing them around her neck. She sat quietly with intensity directed toward the screen on the computer in front of her.

Her co-worker stood with his back to her, a man in his late twenties, in a brown plaid short-sleeve shirt and a dark brown tie, which seemed to match his dark brown hair and beard. His frail body looked as though he rarely, if ever, saw the sun, except for the reflection in the newly polished floor, or from anything other than the inside of this building.

"Excuse me, ma'am?" I said approaching the information desk. "Do you have anything here in regard to the legend of Joseph of Arimathea?"

She looked up and seemed shocked that two "normal" people had asked that question, almost expecting as she had done thousands of times before to see that question coming from strange religious zealots, conspiracy theorists, or doomsday researchers. She motioned to a section of wall across the way.

"All of the books written on the subject of Joseph are in that section, starting at the top," she said. "There is also a room next to the staircase that has a number of videos loaded with some information that you might find interesting. If you would like to do some online research, we have computers over there," she said, pointing to the opposite side of the room. "We just ask for a donation if you want to use the Internet."

"Thank you so much," Gabriela said, and we went toward the bookshelf with the heading "Arimathea."

The shelf was certainly filled with any book you could imagine along the topic of Joseph of Arimathea. Books relating to the legends, folklore surrounding who he was, what his relationship was with Jesus, his occupation, his journeys to England, those who believed he was an alien, others who claimed he was Jesus himself, and more that said it was all a hoax, an attempt to drive visitors to the area.

Gabriela and I shifted through book after book, trying to locate anything about Joseph, Thame Aira, a medallion, anything.

"I would image that if Joseph traveled here on business, wouldn't he have had a contact? A business partner? Someone that would have had a more descriptive history of Joseph's dealings here in England?" I asked Gabriela with a certain amount of exhaustion in my voice, having thumbed through twenty to thirty books at this point.

"Excuse me. I don't want to intrude," came a soft voice with an Australian accent. We looked up and saw a tall nun, who I would imagine was in her late forties.

"No intrusion at all," I said.

"My name is Sister Victoria," she said in a whispered voice even more quiet than the library voice as she pulled out a chair next to us then sat down.

"Sister, what can we do for you?" Gabriela asked.

"I don't know if it's so much what you can do for me, but more of what I can do for you," she said.

Gabriela and I looked at each other as Sister Victoria continued. "Please allow me to explain. All of us sisters here in the library today are from the Order of the Holy Thorn. We have existed for almost six hundred and fifty years; the order, I reference," she said with a slight laugh.

"We spend a lot of time researching various areas of church history, trying to protect and preserve different locations, stories, documents, and artifacts. We are here in Glastonbury to do some research about Joseph, whom you spoke of. Our order," she said holding the pink-colored rope for us to see, "is based in an Abbey near Cambridge, but we are scattered all around the world. I am one of only thirty-six sisters in the order, and I am serving in the abbey in South Africa." She reached back to the nape of her neck and slowly pulled out an additional crucifix made of a silver metal; the crucifix was encircled by a crown of thorns.

"Our order, the Order of the Holy Thorn, is signified by the CMP on the cross, meaning 'crataegus monogyna praecox', and the hawthorn bush used by those who defiled our Lord (she crossed herself) and then brought to England by Joseph."

"Sister Victoria, you have a history with the Glastonbury tradition?" Gabriela asked.

"Yes. You see, we were founded by Elizabeth de Clare, who lived in the abbey at Cambridge. She is said to have kept a secret hawthorn bush in the middle of an exquisite rose garden. Although no one is sure, it is believed that she had some connection with the legend of Joseph. We have searched and searched but have not been able to connect any of the dots. The man whom you search for, his name is Maracleas, a Roman whom lived in this area during the life of our Lord. There is a poem that references his existence, written hundreds of years ago, but it is tucked away in an area in the abbey library here at Glastonbury. It is almost impossible to get to it," she said with a frustrated look to her face.

"Sister Victoria," I said, looking around noticing that other sisters had begun looking in our direction. "Why are you telling us all of this information? Couldn't you get in trouble or lose your standing in the order? If there are only thirty-six of you, I would imagine it is very exclusive and sacred; your work, I mean."

She reached out across the wooden table that divided us, taking one of our hands in each of hers. "I have spent my life as a nun, my entire adult life trying to solve the question of our benefactor, Elizabeth de Clare, and her connection to Joseph. My heart tells me that yours are pure, that maybe this quest needs new eyes and a new perspective; someone like the two of you," she replied.

"We are sorry. I am Gab...."

Sister Victoria held up her hand. "I think for now, it is best to not know who you are. If you are interested, meet me tonight at 9:45 pm at the well of the abbey. I will show you what I can. I hope to see you there." She rose, then crossed herself and moved across the museum.

"Well, that was kind of unusual don't you think?" I said, looking at Gabriela as she sat back in her chair trying to figure out what had just happened.

"I am not even sure what to make of it," Gabriela replied.

"So where are we going to be at 9:45 pm tonight?" I asked.

"I am thinking at a well near the abbey. But what I want to know right now would be, who is this Maracleas character?" Gabriela answered.

The next half hour or so was spent looking for anything in the museum library about Maracleas, and anything that might put the story of Joseph of Arimathea together. Through legends and stories, fairy tales and fables, folklore and myth, we looked at sources, compared versions, and then Gabriela said, "Let's go look online."

"I'll be right over," I said, throwing my wallet to her.

"What's that for?" she asked.

"Making a donation toward the Internet," I laughingly answered.

Maracleas was only referenced in one book that I could find, a book written in 1715 by William Pershall that referenced Maracleas of Naples, who had traveled to Jerusalem in 15 A.D. on business to seek out the needs of Roman officials in the area of metals. It was tin that they needed, tin to mix with copper to make bronze. Tin he knew was available in England, but getting it out had been a problem. Maracleas had made up in his mind to go to England and use his Roman influence to make some money. But what about Joseph? Were they connected at all, or were they complete strangers? I looked up to see Gabriela walking toward me.

"Kiss me," she said as she sat down next to me. I obliged. "Don't you want to know why?" she asked.

"I don't think I need a reason," I said in return.

"You will never believe what I just found out!" she said.

45 AD

The night was black, as dark as any he had seen. Even the moon was painted black by the clouds across the sky. But he had been here before, so he paused and waited for the signal. This trip was so different from the ones in the past, and his heart had been beating harder than normal since leaving Acre. The leather bag thrown over his shoulder had not been taken off during the long two-week journey, and members of the crew thought that he had either started to grow a bit crazy or paranoid, but they trusted him without question, so when they were told of their latest trip, only with half of the normal crew, they looked puzzled but did not ask why.

The coastline's black outline stood out against the night sky, and from a mile out the single lantern lit on the bow of his boat would be hard to see with the naked eye. And so he sat and waited. A half hour passed in silence, seeming to take forever. The constant beating of waves rocking the boat kept time like a sea-born pendulum, and the wood of the mast and deck creaked and groaned like an orchestra of out of tune violins, playing to an empty theater.

A light flashed on shore. Or did it? The looking glass was brought to his face, and he watched as one single light illuminated from the shore. Then after it went out, the signal was official.

"It is time," he said. "Get the boat ready. We are going ashore."

The light on the bow of the boat was extinguished, and the row boat was lowered into the water for the short trip ashore. The constant waves crashing against the shore's sand and rocks grew with intensity as they got closer, and then the dark coast lit again with a single light.

"Light the lantern," he said, and the first rower lit their own light in return. The small rowboat drove hard into the sandy beach and both lights were extinguished for the last time that night. The sound of feet landing in the sand of the beach, followed by the rushing of feet running through sand and over the rustle of rocks, together stopped all at once.

"Joseph, it is so good to have you here. The trip was a good one, I take it?"

"It was. I am blessed to be here safely. It is so good to hear your voice. What would I do without you Maracleas?" Both men turned and walked off the beach into the darkness.

~

Our car pulled up to the abbey parking lot. I whispered to Gabriela, "Are you ready?"

"Why are we whispering?" she asked.

I laughed and then opened the door. The parking lot was full. The sun had almost completely set and the evening was in the very last stages of dusk. Tall candle-shaped lights on poles lit a dim path to the abbey's central hall, and we could hear music. An organ played softly a piece of music by Handel, with the glorious voices joining louder and louder with each note and stanza played.

I took Gabriela's hand and walked across the abbey grounds toward the well. We had prepared at the museum by looking up the layout of the ancient abbey, learning exactly where we should be going. Our thought was, if we're meeting a nun in secret, we should be as prepared as possible.

The grounds were open and airy, with most of the trees surrounding the main abbey hall. The well stood off about three hundred feet from the ancient building. It had felt as Gabriela and I approached that we were alone, with the rolling hills past us lying quiet now that the sun had set.

Almost as if from an Alfred Hitchcock movie she came, walking slowly out of the darkness, the figure of a nun, a tall, slender nun. First it was the dark silhouette of the rolling hills, and then it was as if she grew, rising up from those darkened hills, her habit and robe growing taller and taller against the dark horizon.

"Good evening," she said with the same quiet hush that she had exhibited in the museum.

"Good evening, Sister Victoria," I said.

"I wondered if you would come," she replied.

"We wouldn't have missed this for the world," Gabriela added.

"Can I ask you a question?" I asked.

"Why, of course," Sister Victoria replied, holding her hands together lightly, wrapping the pink rope around her fingers.

"What would the other sisters in the order think about whatever it is that you are thinking about showing us tonight?" I asked. "I mean, you have a secret order. Now you are sharing something with us."

"I understand," she answered. "This could be a clue to something that is nothing, or something amazing. We need to find out."

She glanced toward the abbey. "The concert isn't going to last much longer. We must hurry."

We walked quickly to our car; Sister Victoria sat in the front seat.

"This was found in the abbey library behind a false door," she said.

A small scroll eight inches wide was pulled out of Sister Victoria's robe, and then she pulled it open and read:

Oh Conqueror, Oh Conqueror

The treasure thou didst hide

Among the stones of righteousness

The walls do strength provide.

As Maracleas on England's sod

First found his life, the Son of God

In Living Waters

Dips his Hands

To Wash away the sins of Man

My Lord, My God

I seek you now

On bended knees I see

Looking down, then up into your face

In secret humility.

EDCBA

Gabriela and I looked at each other in amazement. She took out her laptop and copied down the text, and I took photos of it to view later for any details missed. The scroll was rolled again, replaced in Sister Victoria's robe, and she slid me phone numbers, both one here in England and one for her abbey in South Africa.

"Call me. You will know when," she said.

And the door was opened and Sister Victoria stepped out of the car and melted away into the darkness.

Chapter 20

I had been right. Glastonbury had been the best thing for Gabriela. We talked the entire time as we drove back to our hotel, and all the while I thought about a new energy I saw in her; Marco seemed to be a distant memory to her, although possibly she was masking the emotions that lay under the surface, ready to crawl through the cracks at a moment's notice. I wondered about what triggers might remind her of his antics, and what if anything I could do to help her through this time.

Then there was the poem...the writing...whatever it was. What did it all mean? We could look at it in the hotel later.

Gabriela walked from the bathroom, her hair pulled up in a light ponytail, wearing a satin opaque robe that fell to her mid-thigh. She ran her tongue over her freshly brushed teeth inside her lips then said, "What should we do now? I am thinking another trip to the museum? Watch some of the videos? What do you think?"

"I think we need to sleep and think about all of this in the morning," I said falling backward into the pillows on the bed.

I have always thought that the best way to wake up is to do it naturally. No alarm clocks, no trash collectors driving below, no kids jumping on the bed and no phone calls. It is the regaining of conscientiousness, comfortable in your body position, the sheet and blankets are just right, you're not too warm and not too cold, and you open your eyes rested, and you are awake. Gabriela and I woke up perfectly.

Glastonbury Abbey was something completely different during the day than it had been for us the night before. I recognized the wisdom in Sister Victoria wanting to meet with us at night. The "fire in the belly" that she had lit in Gabriela and I was too strong last night. It needed a night for the flames of our eagerness to die down a bit, a half of a day to take the information on the scroll and stew about it. Just like one of my father's cooking creations, letting all the information simmer together, coming out as one savory bite.

The grounds to the abbey were much larger than I could have imagined, and Gabriela and I took our places as tourists, not detectives, because that is exactly what we were—tourists. It was the feeling of being a lover of art, arriving at the Sistine Chapel for the first time only on a time-sensitive shortened visit while on *The Amazing Race* TV show, there for a brief moment to find a hidden clue.

Gabriela and I strolled on at a quickened pace, stopping at various places of interest around the abbey grounds taking pictures along the way. Gabriela was in heaven, not only basking in the mystery that we seemed to be involved in, but also in awe of this abbey, which, depending on who you talked to, had its origins from almost two thousand years before.

The abbot's kitchen was one of the structures that caused Gabriela's heart to leap. It was an octagonal building built in the 1300s, considered by many to be one of the best-preserved medieval kitchens in Europe.

"Jonah, look at this!" Gabriela said grabbing my hand, pulling me along like a rag doll flailing behind her. "Look at the curved buttresses and the gargoyles."

I had no idea what she was talking about, although I had remembered seeing a gargoyle-esque character when stopping for drinks earlier in our trip. She continued talking, instructing me about the architectural ins and outs of this kitchen and the whole site like I was a student with my master teacher on a field trip, minus the sack lunch and Capri Sun.

The inside workings of the kitchen did fascinate me, with the four ovens inside, one in each corner of the building. We continued working our way around the ruins, and then it came into view, the marking of the grave sites for the legendary King Arthur and Queen Guinevere, the sight of which made my throat constrict.

Only once in my life had I felt an emotional connection to a burial site, and that had been George Washington's, causing me to stand in front of my first president's resting spot as tears had welled up in my eyes.

I had normally avoided grave visiting cemeteries, but mostly to visit the graves of my own family. I had on repeated occasions threatened my own children that if after I passed from this life, they were not to visit my grave side. If they did, I had warned them that I would haunt them.

But King Arthur, or Arthurus, as he was called in Latin, with his love, his Queen Guinevere, lying in this holy place, it seemed to be part of my own death. A lifetime of reading, studying about this man, this legend had almost seemed in my mind to have an unattainable ending, like what had happened to Amelia Earhart, was there really a Bigfoot, did the forceful power of the Bermuda Triangle really exist? Where was Noah's Ark?

Here lying in the holy grounds of Glastonbury, lay some other man's Noah's Ark, some other woman's city of Atlantis, and it felt at least for part of me a book had closed in my own mind. Now I could move on. Arthur did exist. He was at peace.

We moved slower now, each of us having been emotionally and in a way spirituality fed with what we had experienced there, and our experience was nothing that we had thought we would experience. I thought about how that was how life worked at its best. We always have things happen to us when we least expect it, when we aren't looking for the blessing; that's when we are blessed.

I had come to England to relax and enjoy some quiet time alone, taking pictures and experiencing this place that had become part of me over years, another Jonah dimension. And I had found Gabriela and a treasure hunt, the two things I desired above anything else in my life; someone who loved me and a treasure to find. Now here they were right in front of me; me being blessed. Then I remembered, the treasure hadn't been found yet, and I had known Gabriela for five days. I would accept those blessings, even in partiality.

"Oh Conqueror, oh Conqueror, the treasure though didst hide; among the stones of righteousness, the walls do strength provide," Gabriela repeated, with no need for prompting or assistance.

"Did you memorize that?" I asked, looking at her with astonishment.

"I never told you?" she asked. "I have kind of a photographic memory!"

"Well that's good to know," I said.

"What do you think it means?" she asked looking at me.

"Well, let's try to break it down a bit. First of all, the fact that the scroll was found here at Glastonbury should play into this. Conqueror. That could be William the Conqueror, with a hidden treasure of...." I trailed off, not knowing of any hidden treasure, although the medallion was in fact buried in a wall, inside a stone.

"The Conqueror could reference Jesus Christ. He is the conqueror of our sins. Isn't that right, Ms. Catholic girl?" I asked Gabriela laughing.

"Yes, yes he is," she answered. "But what treasure would he have hidden, and in what stones of righteousness?"

I thought back to my own Christian upbringing and the verse in the Bible where Jesus tells Peter, "Thou art Peter, and upon this rock will I build my church."

"The treasure could mean eternal life, and the secret to it is hidden in the church. 'Thou art Peter, and upon this rock will I build my church?'" I asked.

"So maybe the rocks of the poem are figurative?" Gabriela asked.

"It could be," I answered, raising my eyebrows and puckering my lips, having no idea. "What is the next stanza?" I asked.

"As Maracleas on England's sod, first found his life, the Son of God. In living waters, dips his hands to wash away the sins of man," she answered back, and then continued. "Maracleas here in England, has been away from Jerusalem and isn't familiar with the phenomenon of Jesus. He hasn't had an opportunity for conversion. So if he found his 'life,' the Son of God on England's sod would seem to me to represent his conversion after the crucifixion of Christ. 'In living waters dips his hands.'"

She stopped and looked at me. "Living waters," I said trailing off in thought.

"Let's go to the well," she said.

We had stopped walking and sat in the arch way of St. Mary's Abbey ruins, almost as if our brains required all of the energy we could provide. The summer morning was warm and still, with various birds hopping through the acres of grass looking for a mid-morning snack. Deep in thought, it was like my brain had focused so much on trying to solve the riddle/puzzle that my senses had become heightened, ultra-sensitive. The sound of the pigeons flapping their wings and flying away echoed louder through the abbey remains. The shrieking of a distant child in delight of being chased by their parent sounded next to me.

"Dipping his hands in living waters," I spoke quietly. "You know that one of the legends of this place is the well. They believe that there is a healing power in the water."

Gabriela added, "And there is a stone wall around the well. I saw that yesterday when I was looking up this place online."

We walked quickly toward the well. "What is the last stanza?" I asked.

"My Lord, my God I seek you now, on bended knees I see. Looking down then up into your face, in secret humility," she repeated.

The well at the abbey at Glastonbury was never really built. It had just existed, like the North Star, the Southern Cross, the Grand Canyon or the Moon. But someone, at some point, came along to beautify it or direct it, like trying to paint the moon. Christian pilgrims began coming to Glastonbury for the healing and supernatural effects provided by the constant flowing spring around 1100 AD, but Pagans and Druids had been using it for centuries.

The spring rose up from the ground with an elaborate metal grate covering the opening that rose from the depths of the earth. The decorative grate was created in the shape of a large circle, with two smaller circles interlocking inside the larger sphere. A sword then pierced through the space shared by the intersecting circles, with an ornate flower design around the outside circle completing the design. Across the path was a wall standing about five feet tall with a stone lion's head protruding out from the stone structure, with the ancient spring moving from the mouth of the beast. The water from the fountain, uncollected for souvenir bottles or drinking, ran down collecting in a pool.

"This is incredible," I said to Gabriela as we approached the well.

"It is absolutely gorgeous," she replied looking at the pamphlet we received on our arrival. "It says here that this well has been visited for thousands of years for its healing and spiritual powers."

"The garden here is enough to cure, I think," I replied. "OK, so let's put this to the test. What was the last stanza again?"

"My Lord, my God I seek you now," she repeated.

"It has to be referencing Jesus Christ, the Lamb of God. I seek you now," I thought out loud.

Gabriela continued. "On bended knees I see. In prayer? Seeking God?"

I looked at Gabriela while walking around the pond, looking in at the water's edge. "Is there somewhere around here where a person could kneel in prayer?" I continued.

"Looking down, then up into your face," Gabriela added. "Is there a face of God here somewhere?"

"That would make sense," I said as I looked around the grounds.

"In secret humility," Gabriela finished.

"Secret humility," I repeated.

"Humility would be on bended knee, would it not?" Gabriela asked.

"I would think so," I replied, adding, "But what would secret prayer mean? Wouldn't 'secret' mean alone, where it is quiet? Maybe when no one was watching?"

Gabriela thought aloud. "If someone was praying here, at this place in secret looking around into the face. Would it be at night? No one would be here, at least not as many as would be here during the day. You could find some privacy, some secrecy."

"What would be different at night?" I asked. "What would we find at night?"

"I have no idea," Gabriela replied.

I finished shooting pictures of the beautiful gardens, the wall, and the well. "Well, should we come back tonight?" I asked.

"I think that we should." Gabriela added, "But while we have the sun, maybe we need to figure out where a person would need to be kneeling at night."

We spent the next while looking at the grounds and finding a lion's head, and calculating where someone would need to kneel to look up into his face. By what we could tell, it would be in the steady stream of cool water draining from his mouth.

"Let's come back tonight, maybe in a pair of shorts," I said

"Seriously?" she asked.

"Seriously," I answered.

I found myself at first looking at my watch, wishing that the evening would quickly arrive, but then I realized that we had an entire day to explore, and why wish a day away? The evening would be here soon enough.

One of the greatest things I was finding out about England was its size. For someone who had grown up in the American West, England was tiny. Driving from one side of the country to the other was a long afternoon drive. We drove to Bath so that Gabriela could show me the architectural wonders of her ancestors. And I could once again watch in awe this master teacher at work.

Chapter 21

The head lights to our car faded out to black shortly after I turned off the ignition. The streets around Glastonbury Abbey were quiet, with the energy of the city seemingly tied to the brightness of the sun. The city was almost asleep now.

Gabriela had slept on our drive back from Bath, and I couldn't blame her. The past week had felt like a month. We had been on the go for most of the entire time. There was the mental strain of this newly found treasure and it had exhausted me as well. Then there was Marco and the emotional beat down that he had put on her. I was sure that his presence was still being felt, especially on the inside. On the way back to Glastonbury I had developed a plan for Marco. When the time was right I would see how she felt about it.

The evening air had held its warmth, right about seventy-five degrees, I imaged, so the thought of immersing myself in a large basin of water wasn't as bad as I thought that it could be, although the temperatures were still dropping. If there was one thing that I had never figured out, it was how a guy like me, raised in the Rocky Mountain Northwest, and then in Boston, hated cold so much but had chosen to live in bitter cold winter zones. Then I reminded myself, this is a quick dip in a summer pond. This isn't the North Sea in January.

My phone rang to the tone of "Skinamarinkadink," letting me know that Lilly was calling; it reminded me of better days with my children, a song that I would sing to them when I put them to bed each night.

"Hey honey" I answered. "How are you? Good. Did you like them? I thought that you would. Well there is more to come, I promise. Do you have any special requests? I think that can be arranged. I love you, too. I will call you in the morning. Bye sweetheart. Tell your brother I love him too. I will...."

"Lilly says 'hi,'" I said to Gabriela as she woke up.

"Ciao," Gabriela said loud enough for Lilly to hear. "Did she get the pictures?" she asked with a huge smile on her face.

"She did and she loved them," I answered, putting my phone on the dashboard. "She just looked at her email and opened them. She loved the pictures from Stonehenge, but you know what her favorite picture is?" I asked.

"The picture of Flat Lilly with those two little toddlers wearing kilts kissing her cheeks," she responded.

Gabriela was right. Gabriela has a talent. Actually, a talent is a trait that comes through practice; she has a gift. She has a very natural ability to walk up to anyone making them feel an instant comfort with her. She would notice the people or situations that I could see as a great photo, and make it happen. I saw two little boys in kilts, thinking out loud what a great picture that would make with Lilly, and Gabriela's gift was to turn what I wanted into a reality. We made a pretty good team, I thought.

"Actually, can you put that in your purse?" I asked, handing the phone to Gabriela. "We are going to need some photos, I think."

"Are you serious about this?" Gabriela asked. "I mean, you are wearing a pair of running shorts and an old T-shirt. This could look strange to anyone who might see you dripping wet when you're done."

"Not as strange as if I were to walk out of there dripping wet with a pair of jeans and a dress shirt," I joked. She looked at me and understood.

The Abbey grounds were now quiet and solemn. It seemed that they were like this all the time, but now in the quiet still of night the solemnity of the grounds echoed off into the darkness, like a drop of water's growing wave, a butterfly effect. We walked hand and hand toward the well, with the faint sound of the water spouting from the lion's head growing with intensity with each step. It sounded like a fountain in Rome, with small naked cherub angels seemingly in flight, at play with one another. But ours was a lion, the opposite of a meek and humble lamb.

The grounds were dimly lit, with mostly round solar lights outlining the paths and walkways throughout the park and an occasional small spotlight shining up on the ancient ruins. The moon, nearly full, illuminated the pond of gathering water, showing the rippling waves dying out with movement away from the center.

"Well Jonah, here it is. The moment of truth," Gabriela whispered, and I thought the same thing. This was us, especially me, putting the theory of ours to the test. What if there wasn't anything here? What if we in our imagination had made too much of the poem? What if we were just wrong?

I remembered watching a TV special, Geraldo Rivera opening Al Capone's vault, live on TV, and it seemed like hours later, there was nothing. At least, I thought, I have a better-looking Italian involved, and there were no television cameras.

I approached the basin and ran my fingers across the surface of the collected water. "This is not bad," I said. I took off my running shoes; flip-flops would have made too much noise. I imagined leaving this place, being chased by a nun with a yard stick, with the smacking of flip-flops leading her in pursuit of us. Running shoes would be....much quieter.

With a cautious first step I tested my weight in the concrete tub. It seemed secure enough, and then at once I lifted my weight entirely on my right foot, now standing completely in the pool.

"Are you OK?" Gabriela asked.

"Yes, it does feel pretty secure," I answered. Then my left foot was lowered into the water, the level of water raised just below my calves. I turned to Gabriela and smiled. "Well, here's nothing." The poem raced through my mind as I lowered my body down into the tub on my knees, feeling the rush of cool water trickle then cascade over my chest and shorts.

Looking down, then up into your face, I thought to myself. I bowed my head. In a way, this "holy" water seemed to be a baptism, having a waterfall of this ancient spring running over me as I bowed my head leaning forward into the spring.

Looking down, I thought.

I opened my eyes, only seeing the water falling from either side of my head and the pool. *Then up.* I raised my head slowly, watching as if there would be a revelation, a sign of something. Then as my head crested, the water spilled directly into my eyes, causing me to quickly close them, and my hands came to my face to wipe the water from my blurred vision.

There is a scene from a movie—a diver down in the depths of some lake or ocean, struggling to reach the surface, crawling with all of the energy available in his body, seeing a distant light, the sun somewhere beyond the waves of the surface. It is that light that gives them hope, that they can crawl a few more strokes, their held breath can last a few more moments before their lungs are going to explode. Then as they break the surface, the wavering sun comes into focus, clear and bright. The water is pushed from their eyes and the world is again in focus. He can breathe again.

And then I saw it, as I rose looking into the mouth of the lion, the faint sign of light glimmered through the watery distraction over my eyes. My hands broke through my own watery surface, making my sight clearer, with a new focus. The source of light, a faint one, came from the upper surface of the lion's mouth. Its color was a pale pink, hardly noticeable, and I looked closer. It seemed that this faint light was only available to someone who would concentrate on the light, without even knowing they were. As I sat in this holy place my thoughts went to life, and how we oftentimes miss those enlightened events because we aren't looking for them. And I had seen the light.

"Hey are you OK?" Gabriela asked. "It looks like you saw a vision or something."

I turned to her. "There is something in the mouth of the lion: a light," I said.

"I don't see a light," she replied, moving around the pool trying to see another angle to look from.

My hand felt up in the mouth of the lion, feeling a rounded indent. "There is something up inside here," I said, pushing my fingers up inside. I could feel a rounded piece, not much different in size from the medallion we held, only this one seemed to have grooves or raised surfaces. My wet fingers struggled to grip the surface. Was it supposed to come out? Wasn't that the point of the poem, to have someone find this light? Then it moved. It pushed up inside the mouth higher. It seemed to be loose. My fingers gripped the raised areas on its face and tried to turn it back and forth. The circular object moved only a fraction, but as it was jostled back and forth, it began to loosen. Then as if it had been in place for hundreds of years it gave way, and the medallion fell into my hand and I slipped it into my pocket.

Gabriela extended her hand as I took a step out of the basin, stabilizing my bare foot on the concrete path; the water dripped from my saturated clothing, creating puddles on the sidewalk.

"Can I see it?" Gabriela asked.

"Let's get in the car first," I responded. I looked down at my running shoes, slipped them on and tied them quickly. And then Gabriela and I started walking down the dimly lit path. I moved off into the grass, wondering if anyone had noticed. At least now the trail of dripping water would disappear. I looked around the park to see if anyone was watching. The darkness of the park was outlined with occasional lights across the grounds, almost like a constellation. I could see one new light beginning to grow from about one hundred feet away, and I could see the faint outline of a person. It looked like the silhouette of a nun as I looked toward this figure. Then the flicker of her light disappeared. Her candle was blown out.

A towel was wrapped around my waist, then I sat in the seat of our car. Gabriela reached over, kissed my cheek, and held my hand as we left the side street parking next to the abbey.

"Can I see it?" Gabriela asked. "I can't believe that you haven't looked at it yet!"

"I just wanted to get out of there as quickly as possible," I responded, looking in the rearview mirror noting no cars seemed to follow us. Glastonbury was snoring.

The bedroom of the bed-and-breakfast was simple and plain, with a queen-sized bed decorated with a red comforter, and a few incidental pieces of furniture around the room; but at least it had its own bathroom.

I jumped into a quick shower, relieving myself of the film and smell of the well's water, and the pajama bottoms and dry shirt felt much more comfortable. I decided to brush my teeth now rather than later.

Gabriela sat cross-legged on the bed with a look of amazement, holding in her hands the new medallion.

"Jonah, look at this! It is absolutely beautiful!" she said, with her hand extended toward me, showing the source of the pink light that I had seen an hour before.

I sat down next to her on the bed facing her and took this new medallion in my hands. It was a bit larger than the Battle medallion, but looked to be made of the same material. At first glance I would assume that they had come from the same maker. But this circular medallion was different, like Hawaii and Alaska are both states, but they are just different.

It bore an inscription around its edge in two circles. But what was stunning were the pink stones that were enlarged completely through the face. Small oblong stones formed the outline of a flower, its petals circled within the medallion shaped as crescent moons, inverted V's, and almost rectangular shaped stones.

"The inscription, do you see that?" Gabriela asked. And I read.

"The flower of thorns, doth appear divine,

Like the Son of God, holds the key.

In prose you unlock the origins of life

With the turning of direction, the key."

"Another puzzle?" I said. "But I have to admit this piece is beautiful."

"The flower of thorns doth appear divine," Gabriela read aloud. "This medallion and the pink stones do resemble the bud of the thorn tree, and the markings do appear quite divine," she added.

"Like the Son of God holds the key," I read. "Like the Son of God holds the key. So does the flower, or is it the medallion flower that is holding the key? In prose you unlock the origins of life."

"Poetry," Gabriela added. "With the turning of directions, the key."

I picked up the medallion, examining it from various angles, looking closely at the jewels, holding them up to the light, examining the backside, noticing that nothing was written on its surface. I laid down the medallion, asking Gabriela to read it one more time. Of course, she did it from memory.

"In prose, I think that could be a key," she said.

"I don't know if I can do this anymore!" I exclaimed, laughing then falling back to the bed. Gabriela moved toward me, lying next to me. She kissed me and moved her leg across the bed, knocking the new medallion to the carpeted floor. It rolled.

"Oops!" she blurted.

"Is it OK?" I asked, grabbing her waist with my hands. She glanced at it.

"Yes" she said. It came to rest on a Bath tourism guide that had fallen from her bag.

Gabriela leaned back toward me and kissed me again. Her lips were soft and…"Oh, my! That is it! I know! I know! I know!" she said jumping up, reaching to the floor, falling off the bed in a frantic attempt to get the medallion. She then knelt at the side of the bed holding the medallion and the tourist paperwork together. "They go together," she said.

"They go together?" I asked.

"Yes, yes, yes," she shouted. "Not the medallion and the…the this," she said, holding up the brochure. "The medallion and the poem. They go together."

Gabriela jumped on the bed, laid the Bath paperwork on the bed in front of us, and then set the medallion over the text. "You see. It will decipher only certain words from the original poem, saying something else to us. It's the stones. They will allow only the words we need to know through!"

"In prose you unlock the origins of life," I repeated. "With the turning of direction, the key. What is the turning of direction?"

"We need to print the poem to its exact size. How big was it?" she asked.

"I think about six by eight," I answered.

"We need to print it exactly the same size or we will not get the right words," she said.

"We can print the photo I took, but I don't think there are any Walmart stores or copy shops open right now. Plus, I think we want to do this without anyone seeing it. Don't you think?" I added.

"We can find something in the morning." Gabriela responded. "I think we need to get some sleep. It's 1:24 am."

The bed was comfortable; soft enough but firm enough as we lay holding each other. I stroked her hair, and held her tight against me.

My mind went back to Lilly and Dawson and my relationship with them, singing to them each night before bed, and reciting an occasional poem, my favorite, "Wynken, Blynken and Nod," by Eugene Field, and I began to recite it quietly to Gabriela.

"Wynken, Blynken, and Nod, one night sailed off in a wooden shoe;
Sailed off on a river of crystal light, into a sea of dew.
'Where are you going and what do you wish?' the old moon

asked the three.
'We've come to fish for the herring fish that live in this
beautiful sea;
Nets of silver and gold have we,' said Winkin', Blinkin', and
Nod."

And I heard Gabriela breathing softly, asleep, finally
succumbing to the undeniable pull of Glastonbury's slumber, and I
closed my eyes and fell asleep.

Chapter 22

The Glastonbury downtown area seemed more vibrant than it had been the previous couple days. Crowds were filling the streets with all varieties of people. The holiness of this place spoke to every sect. As we walked we were an audience to a variety of sidewalk musicians playing their own unique brand of music. Irish children, dressed in their customary outfits, danced and sang an Irish jig as others played the instruments of fiddle and flute. There were guitar soloists, bagpipers, street drummers, flutists, and even a string quartet playing *Adagio for Strings*, by Samuel Barber.

It was the beginning of the Glastonbury Music Festival, and it seemed that it was time for the city to wake up; having been in a Brigadoon dream, only these residents came to life once a year.

There were some religious fanatics warning of the end of times, the one-world conspirators, those protesting war, or begging for help with world hunger. Some were against the killing in the Sudan, and of course that our world was suffering from heat exhaustion and was melting away. "Ride a bike, starve a fever," their songs proclaimed.

We found street vendors selling everything, but my eyes found the world-famous Scottish deep-fried Mars bars. I had seen them on one of those traveling shows on the Discovery Channel. Gabriela and I shared one. It was an acquired taste, I decided. A flyer was being handed out outlining today's acts on the main stage. At noon was Lenny Marley, the son of Bob, 2:00 pm Coldplay, 4:00 pm Simple Minds, 6:00 pm Rihanna, and 8:00 pm U2.

"What do you say? Are you up for a day off?" I asked.

"I would love one," Gabriela responded.

~

The train came to a stop. The SV-317 arriving from Land's End seemed to appear from a land that time had forgotten. Steam released from the engine's pleated front like the breath of a horse on a cold winter's day.

"Ten o'clock service from Glastonbury to Liverpool by way of Birmingham, prepare to board in ten minutes," a jovial rail agent barked out in a very cordial way. Gabriela lifted her head from my shoulder as we sat in a small waiting area with ten other passengers.

The day had been filled with festivities for anyone. Music blared from the main stage and the variety of other stages around Glastonbury. Gabriela and I spent the day walking, enjoying a day of sunshine, arts-and-crafts vendors, foods of all varieties, and a relaxing quick nap in the park.

"How are you feeling?" I asked.

"I am having a great time," she answered with a smile beaming from her face.

"No really, I don't want to intrude, but are you thinking about Marco? Are you still worried about him being out there somewhere?" I asked.

"He is always in my mind on some level or another. There are moments when I see something and it strikes a stake of fear in my heart, but there are times when he is a universe away," she replied.

I contemplated how to ask this. "What if we could get him away from here for at least the time being?" I asked.

She looked at me with a quizzical look.

"I've been thinking. What if we could get him detained...so to speak?"

So at 4:00 pm, I went into the cheapest hotel we could find and paid for a room for the night.

At 4:15 pm, I took Gabriela's phone, reconnected the battery, and inserted the phone between the mattress and the box springs.

At 4:25 pm, I left the hotel, heading out into the parking lot where Gabriela was waiting.

At 4:35 pm, Gabriela and I went across the street to a restaurant and ordered an early dinner and sat at a window table and waited.

At 5:29 pm, we watched Marco's automobile pull into the parking lot.

At 5:33 pm, we called England's emergency number, 999, to notify them that someone could be trying to break into our motel room, Salisbury Suites room 219.

At 5:55 pm, Marco was taken from the motel, handcuffed and arrested, charged with trespassing, illegal entry, destruction of property, and assault of a constable.

At 6:10 pm, we went back to the motel, signed the necessary paperwork, and went back into the room, noticing the door frame being torn apart. We collected my bag of wet clothes from the night before and Gabriela's phone, still tucked away inside the bed.

At 6:15 pm, we went and told the staff that we really didn't feel safe staying there; they obliged and refunded the room rate, and offered a free night's stay in one of their chain of motels (which I felt guilty taking) and asked what else they could do.

"Do you have a computer room with a printer?" I asked.

At 6:23 pm, Gabriela and I walked out of the Salisbury Suites with fifteen copies of "The Poem," all in a little different size.

At 7:45 pm, we stood in the back of a mass of one hundred thousand people watching Rihanna and then U2 from about what seemed like a kilometer away.

At 8:20 pm, I looked up Brit rail ticket information and bought two tickets to Edinburgh, Scotland. The train was departing in almost two hours.

The sun had shown brightly all day, although the temperature was probably never higher than eighty-five degrees, but the redness it produced on my neck and parts of my face was undeniable. This was a sunburn.

"I have something I can put on your burn," Gabriela said with a look of pain, and then grabbed her bag that contained a little bit of everything.

"I am not a big fan of lotions, of any kind," I said. "They are all greasy and sticky and...."

She cut me off by putting her finger to my mouth. "Hush child, you are going to be all right. I promise," she said with a hushed whisper.

The train compartment was something I would have pictured in Agatha Christie's *Murder on the Orient Express*. It was an area of about eight feet by six feet, with two bench seats facing each other, each with a comfortable maroon suede back and seat. Dark wood trimming accented the walls and door to the washroom, which was directly to the left once walking in through the sliding door.

A gentle knock on the glass from the porter took our attention to him sliding the door open.

"Tickets, please. May I collect your tickets?" he said with a warm smile. I couldn't tell if he really loved his job as a seventy-something year old, or if he was forced back into the workforce like a greeter at Walmart. "We will be departing shortly to Birmingham, arriving there in just a tad under an hour. Then we will be in Liverpool at half past midnight. I see that you are extending your travels up to Edinburgh. You will be switching trains in Liverpool for the remainder of your voyage north. Is there anything I can do for you?" he asked, like he had repeated this spiel a million times.

"I think we are good," I said.

"Oh, there are blankets and pillows in the compartment under the seats, and if you push in," he pushed the seat of the bench toward its own wall, then it clicked out, "it will then pull out into a cozy little bed," he finished.

"Thank you," Gabriela answered.

He pulled the door window shade down, locking it into its hooks, and started sliding the door shut. "Have a nice trip, folks."

The bed pulled out smoothly, with the back sliding down into place. Gabriela went in and did whatever she does in the washroom and I pulled a few blankets and pillows out creating a place for us to relax. The train pulled out of the Glastonbury station and cut through the British night, with its darkened landscape and dots of lights spread like a regime of fireflies along the way. It was an area that I wanted to see during the day, heading north with the Welsh countryside to the west, and England to our east. *No use changing any clothes, we are going to be on this train for a couple of hours,* I thought. Then the door opened and Gabriela walked out.

She had this ability to draw your complete attention everywhere she went. And she certainly had mine. Her curly hair was pulled over each shoulder, hanging down in front of her chest, covering a loose-fitting tank top that matched pink sweat bottoms that completed her look of comfort.

She slid toward me across the bed, resting her back against my drawn-up thighs, then pulled her knees up against my waist and I kissed her until Birmingham. And then we kissed until Liverpool.

The train we boarded in Liverpool had a much more twenty-first century feel than the train from Glastonbury. It was cleaner, yet less personable, sleeker but unromantic, and instead of it being a horse breathing through the English countryside, we now rode a bullet shooting off into the darkness.

"I can't sleep," Gabriela said in a sleepy voice.

"I can't either," I replied.

Our private cabin felt more like a cheap motel on tracks, with a bit more comfortable bed than that in our cabin to Liverpool. I had decided to get more comfortable, throwing on a pair of shorts and getting out of the shoes and socks that had been on my feet all day. It felt good to just lay with Gabriela in my arms and relax, although the photocopies of the poem and the new medallion were on my mind. But we had decided for twenty-four hours to take a break. Marco was in custody. The Glastonbury police would call me if that changed. Our past six days had felt like we were standing in the median of the Los Angeles freeway playing Frogger, trying to cross. The action had been non-stop. It was concluded that we needed time, for us, for our bodies, and for our brains, all to relax and breathe. And so we started on the train to Scotland doing just that, hearing the occasional heartbeat, shallow inhale and exhale of oxygen, and the constant humming of our train against the tracks beneath us. And Gabriela was asleep.

It would be five hours to Edinburgh. It was time to relax and sleep. I turned on the small TV monitor snuggled away nicely on the wall next to the bed. It had been a while since I looked for a baseball score. Now would be a perfect time.

It was 1977, and the Los Angeles Dodgers were playing the hated New York Yankees in the World Series. As a kid growing up in the American Northwest, the closest team to cheer for was the newly-founded Seattle Mariners, or the San Francisco Giants or Oakland A's. I suppose I was a kid who jumped on the nearest bandwagon, and so it was and would always be my Los Angeles Dodgers. Moving to Boston with the Red Sox as a Dodger fan was a lot like living in France during World War II, then moving to England. You had a common enemy in Germany and Adolph Hitler; Boston and I had the New York Yankees.

ESPN showed highlights of a day game between the Dodgers and the Milwaukee Brewers, with Matt Kemp hitting another home run—twenty-seven for the season—and L.A. extending its lead in the National League West to eight and a half games over San Diego.

They haven't faltered since I've been gone. Perfect, I thought, thinking I had some kind of control of the team with my own actions.

I thought about the poem and the reverse alphabet on the bottom, almost as if it were the signature of the author. "EDCBA." It seemed odd almost trying to say something through it alone. The poem text was scripted in a standard medieval written font, but the alphabet was different, written in a signature script, but still printed and separated. I decided to shoot off a quick email to my college friend, Dr. Bowles, to see if he could do something with it.

I typed with one thumb on my phone.

"Russ. Found a poem written, but seems to be signed, EDCBA. Any thoughts? Jonah."

I put my phone away, slid down directly behind Gabriela, and she backed directly into me, burrowing in with a slight shake of her body. She was asleep.

Baseball, baseball, baseball, I thought.

1345

It had been fifteen years in the making; a large percentage of her own lifetime had been involved.

I am done....finally, *she thought,* It is out of my hands now. The last piece is in place. I am not an artist or a poet; I do not claim to occupy the mind of a mathematician, creating clues and puzzles to solve this. Only the imagination of a woman who wants sacred things kept sacred. I have done my part, at least what I thought was best. I only hope it was enough. May the finder of these clues possess Faith, Love, Humility, and Forgiveness, and possess within their heart the gift of healing.

Elizabeth then signed the document, EDCBA, rolled up the scroll, crossed herself as she stood in the abbey at Cambridge, tucked the scroll inside her satchel and went outside to the carriage and driver that awaited her.

"My lady. What is your pleasure?" the driver asked.

"Geoffrey, we are heading to Glastonbury," she replied.

Chapter 23

Forty miles from Edinburgh sits a grove of oak trees situated on the top of a long slope that overlooks the Hamilton valley. The hills around the valley are long and rounded with green for as far as the eyes can see, making it seem like looking over a herd of green camels.

The Cadzow Oaks, as they are called, have seen their own share of history, been climbed by generations of children, and have provided shelter and cover for many a bird, squirrel, hare, and deer from the harsh winds and rains of each and every Scottish storm that rolls in from the frigid North Sea.

The oaks once stood majestically protecting the Cadzow Castle, but after generation and generation, the castle slowly fell into disrepair, crumbling into the faint ruins that remain to this day. But the Cadzow Oaks remained firm, unfaltering.

During the reign of King Edward II of England, there was an Englishman by the name of Walter fitz Alan. He had the distinction of working in Bothwell Castle, an English-controlled castle in the territory of Scotland, as its "general manager," for lack of a better term. During the Battle of Bannockburn, English forces led by Edward II left Bothwell Castle, in preparation for battle against Robert the Bruce, the future King of Scotland, with Walter left in tow to manage the affairs of the castle. The battle raged and victory seemed to move from side to side like a Newton's Cradle, one of those games with five metal hanging balls and the two outside spheres bouncing back and forth.

Eventually momentum fell completely with the side of the Scots, and Edward called for a full retreat. Half of the English army, led by Edward, rode to the coast and down toward London, and the others directly toward the peacefully waiting Bothwell Castle, and Walter fitz Alan.

A watchman along the top of the castle's wall announced the coming arrival of their countrymen in full run. Walter ordered the gate opened and to the great relief of the battered soldiers, an oasis of safety was finally theirs.

Walter fitz Alan pondered for a moment at his newfound predicament.

If my countrymen are retreating on a full gallop, then that can only mean that they've lost and the Scotsmen aren't far behind. *So he did what anyone would do; he helped each soldier out of their gear and kindly escorted them into the awaiting dungeon.* It is a matter of survival and negotiations, *he thought.*

Soon enough, the newly crowned King Robert the Bruce of Scotland road up to Bothwell Castle, full of Englishmen in now Scottish controlled lands again. Walter had the gates opened and invited the king into the Castle.

"Look what I've got for ya; an entire load of Englishman," he said.

A puzzled Robert, looking almost as if pointing at the dungeons and then back at Walter with a look of "What?," finally said to Walter:

"Well, what do you want for them?"

"Well, Your Grace, I was thinking that I would love to have my own castle, with all the rights and titles with it," Walter replied.

"Oh, is that all." *Robert thought,* here he is an Englishman turned traitor against his own men. How can he ever be trusted?

"I'll make a deal with you," *Robert announced.* *"I'll give you the title of Cadzow Castle (a small castle situated next to Robert's most trusted military man) until the time you harvest your first crop."*

That will put him in and out of here within a year's time, *Robert contemplated,* and then nowhere to go.

"Great! I appreciate this very much," *Walter exclaimed, kneeling down in front of King Robert, and he kissed his ring.*

Then in a twisted turn of events, Walter fitz Alan and his son, Alan fitz Walter, agreed to harvest....wood; in fact, oak, which takes at least fifty years to grow. And without anything to say to him, but to only keep a watchful eye, King Robert knew he had been taken and he rode off to manage his new country; not a good start, *he thought,* but then he laughed to himself.

Walter and Alan planted their oak trees, soon to be known as the Cadzow Oaks.

Seven hundred years later, a small car drove along a distant road. Gabriela and Jonah drove toward the grove of trees in central Scotland: the Cadzow Oaks.

Chapter 24

There were no historical posts along the road marking the way to Cadzow, but I knew the general area with maps that I had brought of how to get to them. We pulled our car off onto a gravel side road and watched as a Scottish sheep herder with a seven-foot staff in hand and two trusted dogs managed a much mangier looking herd of sheep than what we had experienced to the south.

As we watched the herdsman, there was something about him that spoke of simple majesty, a proud man, a hardworking man who had spent his life on the land working the tools of his trade.

He leaned against his staff, his head pressed against his hands, with a wind and sun-ravaged face that peered out over his herd, I imagined with thoughts of his wife at home, his children at school, and what he needed to do yet this year to get the sheep ready for market. He was an American cowboy, only in Scotland with sheep.

I had grown up with that quintessential American cowboy, never wanting that lifestyle for myself, but respecting those who did. They were the backbone of the American West, bringing to mind John Wayne and Jimmy Stewart in the movie *The Man Who Shot Liberty Valance*—two men in the American West with unique characteristics, but each a necessary bone completing the spine.

The sheep herder's hair was a faded red, from age and the sun. Its disheveled appearance was tucked unmanaged under a Tam o' Shanter, and was followed by a thick red beard; with the green and black kilt with matching sash, his plaid, his tartan, spoke of generational heritage, his family. He wore a cream colored undershirt that provided cover from the sun, and ensemble was completed with his shoes and long socks. I was reminded of the convenience store clerk I had talked to a few short mornings before, and how they both looked almost identical to the naked eye. But as I thought about how similar they were, their deep contrasts stood out even more.

Both were books, well worn from age and abuse, but the convenience store employee was a torn up copy of *An Idiot's Guide to Being a Scotsman* and the herdsman was a first edition copy of Adam Smith's *Wealth of Nations*.

His dogs barked once as we got out of the car, and he yelled to them, not wanting to startle the sheep. He moved with the walk of a man with no place to be in any hurry, but could walk until he would figure it out.

(Incomprehensible language), he said as he got closer to us.

"I'm sorry, what was that?" I asked.

"Oh great, a couple of Yanks we have here, do we? I'll speak a little slower for ya," he smiled. "Are ya lost? Needing some directions?" he said.

"We're that obvious, huh?" I answered back.

"Well, not exactly, at least not until you couldn't understand a thing I was saying to ya....That's when I knew," he said.

The bells of a couple of his sheep rang out, only much hollower and lower sounding than I had ever heard before. The largest of the sheep, a huge ram with rounded horns, a goatee, and long matted wool discolored by the earth, looked at us. He seemed to be "the man." He bleated at us loudly, shook his head and went back to chewing on the green grass, ringing his bell as he moved his neck.

"We are looking for the Oaks, the Cadzow Oaks. I have a map here but I have gotten turned around or something. Not sure what I did wrong," I replied, fumbling through the papers I printed online. I looked up at the herdsman, who had a concrete focus on Gabriela, and she knew it.

"I bet you have all kinds of us tourists out here lost looking for directions. Don't you?" she said to him, knowing that he had slipped under her spell. It made me think of the Roman occupation of this island; it was never quite complete. The Romans were never fully able to command this place, especially Scotland. There was a reason Emperor Hadrian had built a wall between England and Scotland. If he couldn't control them, then build a wall and keep them out. The answer was right here. They didn't need fifty-thousand soldiers; they had needed ten-thousand Gabrielas.

"Well, Cadzow did you say? Is that what you are looking for?" he asked. "Angus, Angus Hamilton is my name. I would share my hand, but Lord knows what it's touched already this morning."

Maybe our books weren't that much different after all, I thought.

"The oaks. Back on the road behind ya, then head north about a minute or two, untale ya see a big ole mule. Ya can't miss em. Turn left before em and then down another kilometer of so, right along the ridge line. Ya really can't miss em," he said.

"I am Gabriela and this is Jonah. Is there anything you've heard about the oaks, any stories or legends?" she asked.

Angus replied. "There is a story that has been going around these parts for quite some time, I think mostly a teenage ghost story. They say that during the first full moon during harvest season, you can go down to the oaks and sit near where the old place stood and hear a man or a couple of men laughing."

"Have you ever heard it?" I asked.

"Personally I haven't, but there was a time a few years back when I was moving a herd of my sheep down past the place, and I know that there was like an invisible fence around the place. My sheep wouldn't even get close to it, even my dogs started to growl, showing their teeth and all. There is a story about animals and them having a deeper instinction or perception of things we know nothing about; things from the beyond and such," Angus continued. "If you're interested in old Nessie, I can't help you there," he said with a chuckle.

"Could we ask you for one more favor?" Gabriela asked reaching over and touching his arm. He would have personally wrestled Nessie out of Loch Ness at that very moment if the body of water had even been close for her.

"I suppose," he replied.

"We are shooting some pictures for an online magazine. Would you mind it if we took some pictures of you and your sheep?" she asked.

"You can shoot all the pictures you want," he answered.

I handed him a business card, pointing to my email address, and he gave me his in return.

"As long as I can get a shot of me and the lady here," he replied. "It is kiltedram@yahoo.co.uk."

It struck me at this moment that Gabriela knew me. She was starting to see part of the world through my eyes. She knew that the image of Angus looking out over the landscape, leaning effortlessly against his staff, would be an image I would want. She knew how I thought and felt and looked at my world more in a few days with me than anyone had in my entire life.

Monica had seen a deep chasm in me, that missing part of me that needed to be crossed over and recovered, but had no ability to reach me. If I had been a gunshot victim, Monica would have called the ambulance, told me everything was going to be OK; stay calm. Gabriela would plug my wounds with her own fingers trying to stop the blood from running out of my body, and not caring if she was as bloody as me, then call for help. I sensed in Gabriela a deeper care and concern, a woman who would read a manual on how to treat gunshot wounds while plugging my holes.

Other women had tried and failed. Some took the approach of chasing down my attacker, leaving me there to bleed. Others used the Band-Aid technique—what you can't see won't hurt you—and then there were more who subscribed to the full open heart approach; the blood pumping out the holes was being driven by a defective heart. A new one was in order. But there was never a worthy donor. It was the gentle touch of her healing fingertips, knowing exactly what to do. And my blood was beginning to stop flowing outward.

We shot some pictures of Angus and his flock of sheep after he had first posed with Gabriela. His sun and wind-worn face stood out as I zoomed in tight from his side and back, catching a faint outline of the Scottish countryside in the background. In his mind he was keeping sacred things sacred. A man, and his land and his sheep.

The Cadzow Oaks, I explained to Gabriela, were part of the family history of a friend of mine, Chris Harrison. I had made a promise to him that I could bring back some pictures. As we approached the remains of the castle we realized that there were none. Every stone had been removed, leaving a faint outline of its foundation that I assumed would be better viewed from above. Thick growth of weeds and fallen branches made up most of the small castle floor. Occasionally we found broken beer bottles, an empty pack of smokes, or an item of clothing left decaying against the ground. The oaks stood firm but gnarly, the sign of seven hundred years of growth, wind, and storm. We took photo after photo of everything; Chris would be thrilled. Gabriela in her architecturologist role started to draw an outline of the old place, putting her skills of pencil and paper together in a way that I could never. I walked around the grounds kicking at rocks, trying to find something that told the story, the story of this castle that hadn't been carried away all these years.

Then it hit me. Sometimes we get so stuck looking at our past, looking backward instead of forward. The holes left in the ground of this place from stones unearthed and carried away gradually were filled over time. They were filled with new life, of fallen new seeds from an old grove of trees; inside the old grow the new. The holes of the earth were gently being replaced by the light touch of the healing seeds. I started picking up the acorns of these oaks, these tiny fingertips of healing, filling a pocket of my camera bag. Chris would love this.

I then began to realize that I needed to allow my own self to forgive and forget my past and allow the fingertips of my own life to fill in any old wounds and create a fresh start.

~

Jonah stood over around the grove of oaks and I wondered what was going through his head. He really was unlike any man that I had ever experienced before. I watched him kick at the ground like a small boy looking for something to play with. The thought came to me that he was. He was a kid at heart and had a love for life, but more than that for living. I could tell that he was guarded, not letting some parts of him out to be exposed to hurt and pain. But I also had experienced in him the most kind, gentle and delicate man, someone that I had subconsciously looked for.

He looked at me as I sketched the foundation to this castle with a smile, and his beautiful blue eyes looked at me with safety and love. I could see that Jonah had a love for me, and as we sat there in this remote deserted place, I could tell that I loved him too. Just being here in this maze of spontaneity was something Marco would have never done, especially out in this dirt and growth. It would have ruined his shoes. It would have gotten in the way of his schedule. Jonah understood me. He looked like someone who had won the lottery, but didn't believe it. He was a beautiful man physically; his dark brown hair curled up in the back and his blue eyes were framed with a few wrinkles. He reluctantly saw himself as attractive, not believing that his lottery ticket was a winner. But I loved it and that about him, a humility that added to his attractiveness. There was a physical draw to him that at times I felt was almost unmanageable, but I had tried to hold back, not wanting this experience to be completely physical. I could tell that he didn't either.

My experience with men was one of them wanting me for my body and what that could provide to them in a variety of ways; an arm to possess at a charity event, someone to show off in public, and sex. My first night with Jonah, when he put me to sleep with the gentle touch of his fingertips rubbing my feet, I immediately could tell he was different, and my own walls started to come down. His hands have contained a unique healing power that has started to transform me. My thoughts drift off at times wondering about what is going to happen in a week. How will we depart? What will happen to us? All I know now is that I want today to last forever and then tomorrow.

~

The work Gabriela created on her sketch pad was phenomenal, outlining this castle that time had almost forgotten if not for the ghostly skeleton of its foundation that lay at rest in the ground. We heard no one laughing that day, no ghosts of the past. We did hear the process of healing beginning. I asked Gabriela if I could buy the sketch.

"Why do you think I drew it? It is a gift for your friend," she said.

I immediately imagined this sketch framed, with one addition: the cap of an acorn placed inside the frame to remind us that with all things past, there is always a new growth, a new beginning. Wounds will heal but you must first plant the healing power of the tiniest seeds.

Chapter 25

Edinburgh, Scotland, was beautiful, and since I had flown into London on my first day, I hadn't experienced a larger city like this once putting London in my rear view mirror. The old Edinburgh was mostly cobblestone streets with stone buildings four to five stories tall with narrow little shops and pubs for every delight. I had become a tourist, which had been the goal here, to be a tourist without falling into the tourist trap things. The Edinburgh Castle sat very eloquently on a hill seemingly looking out over its city, still under its watchful eye. A guide escorted us inside, giving a historical snapshot of the peoples and the events that had taken place here. I could hear the lead actors in this drama with each story told. Gabriela could feel their history as her hands ran over the immaculate stonework that made up this place.

"Isn't it beautiful?" she directed as more of a statement rather than a question.

"It really is," I answered with no question at all.

I watched as tourists from Japan, Australia, Mexico and the U.S. walked along shooting pictures with cameras dangling around their necks, swaying to and from like the pendulum of a grandfather clock, with the exception of a large German woman, very well endowed; her Nikon wasn't going anywhere. *In fact it might get crushed*, I thought.

Gabriela's language skills added uniqueness with her ability to listen and translate most of the languages spoken. I myself want to listen intently and work on my Scottish accent.

"On yer right is a letter from Sir James Sheffield, the eighth Duke of Ness and third Earl of Ulster, thanking King James I for translating the Bible into English in 1603. As you may or may not know, the Bible was only available in Latin before 1603 and if you didn't read Latin, you couldn't read the Bible. It made all who wanted to read the Bible at home much more available. Before that you had to go to mass and listen to your priest or clergyman recite it in Latin," said the guide.

I read the bottom of the letter, signed Sir J. Sheffield 8DN3EU. I took a couple more steps and then I stopped and turned back. Gabriela looked pulling back toward me with our hands still connected.

"Did you see that?" I asked pointing to the initialized signatures.

"Yes, so?" she added.

"That is the answer. EDCBA. It is a signature, maybe not for the sake of saving time but for a clue," I said with excitement in my eyes.

She looked at me as if I were a bit crazy, and maybe I was.

"Twenty-four hours. We are giving ourselves twenty-four hours, remember?" she said.

I smiled. "Let's go catch up," I said, now feeling like Charlie and Grandpa Joe having burped themselves down from the ceiling fans in the chocolate factory. We ran to catch up.

We continued walking through the streets of Edinburgh taking in the sights and sounds. A breeze began to blow, slightly at first, and the clouds gathered together above us and we ducked into a local eatery, 6 Pieces of Silver, established 1753. It was a pub that served food. I was noticing that more and more about this place, and I was sure that at some point we would soon discover a pub that sold women's dresses.

We took a corner table near the front window. It was narrow and deep with a sitting bar along one side and enough room on the other for small tables for four to be staggered enough for walking clearance. The floors were dark brown planks with the wear and distress of hundreds of years in this place. I thought that this is what an Old West saloon floor must have resembled. I could only image the number of times that a glass mug of ale had torn into the wood. How many fights had been started with a chair being broken over someone's back, or even how many times someone went through the glass door spilling onto the street. The walls were painted forest green, and then lined with a variety of Edinburgh Hearts FC soccer jerseys showing the history of the home club, along with pictures of musicians, artists, actors, all here in its history.

The menu was set in front of us at our table, our server named Molly. "Anythun I can get ya started with?" she asked.

Gabriela ordered wine, and I got my customary water. Then I read the front of the menu.

"*Welcome to 6 Pieces of Silver, established 1753. In 1865, a feller by the name of Robbie McEwan came in one night bragging about his six-legged pup that his dog had just delivered. Jimmy McAfee, the proprietor, was serving drinks that night and had a few too many drinks himself and said:*

"Robbie, you're a bloody liar." Robbie answered, "No I tells ya, it's the truth. How much you want to bet?" Jimmy responded, "Bring yer pup here and if it's got six legs, I'll sell you this place for a piece of silver per leg."

The rest is history. And in case yer wondering the reason we told the story on the menu? The bar maids got tired of telling the story. It was pissin them off. Just a warnin, they'll pour a beer on ya if you ask.

Bobby Livingstone, Owner

With that warning we ordered, corned beef and potatoes for me, and for Gabriela, chicken Caesar salad. And in my mind the reverse alphabet ran through it over and over. But I had promised Gabriela that we would restart the "investigation" in the morning. Today was about Gabriela and I and Edinburgh.

Molly arrived with our check; we thanked her and got up to leave when we heard the voice of a German-accented man at the bar. "Why is this place called Six Pieces of Silver?" We both turned to look, and the bar maid picked up a shot glass full of ale and threw it in his face, and the place exploded in applause and cheers.

We walked down the street and the wind continued to blow, and suddenly the rain fell down hard. An alley was to our right and Gabriela ran around the corner, pulling me with her under a weathered green fabric window cover, providing a futile attempt to keep us dry. I pushed Gabriela against the cream painted stone wall for as much protection as I could provide.

"What should we do? Run for it?" I asked.

"Kiss me," she said pulling me into her against the building.

And we did, as passionately as I have kissed anyone. Her lips were soft and moist, and my hand slid around her neck and our bodies pressed against each other feeling like two puzzle pieces that you spent hours trying to match up, finally finding their mate. The wind whipped the weathered cover against the wall, exposing us completely to the elements, but it didn't matter. The rain saturated us. It would have made a great photo had someone been there to take it. But I had in my mind frozen that experience for the rest of my life.

"I love you," she said bringing her hands up to my face, our noses touching each other.

I looked back at her. "I have loved you from the minute I laid eyes on you," I replied with no hesitation.

I wiped the water from her eyes but the rain continued to fall, but the water I missed, she cleared with her fingers in the corner of her eyes. But it wasn't rain; she was crying.

We walked back to the street with our arms folded inside of each other, then turned toward our hotel with the pace of two people with no place to be in any hurry. While the world around us ran quickly past us in search of cover, I was comfortable walking in the rain, feeling its effects washing over my body, with the run-off slowly changing from deep red, then to pink, and eventually running as clear as the Scottish rain. My healing had continued and had I been broken ground, small oak shoots would have been sprouting from my body, from the tiniest seeds.

There are moments in our lives that help define who we are or what is most important to us. I remembered back to situations that I didn't understand in my life, like my friend in high school on a trip to San Francisco wanting to spend the day in a video arcade, or my sister visiting Disneyland only to go to a movie in the park. But now here I was visiting Edinburgh, Scotland, and wanting only to kiss Gabriela. *Who cares about William Wallace*, I thought. This dream of mine, finding the woman of my dreams, I remembered had begun with Miss Dorius, my fourth grade teacher. My love of history had been a slow learning process, but finding the woman of my dreams had been in my heart much longer. This reality was not what I had imagined as a fourth grader. Miss Dorius never looked like this. She was not Gabriela.

Chapter 26

The dark clouds had hung over England all day. Completely covering the sky, the clouds had held the sun at bay, with only the slight changing from dark to light and then back to dark again signifying the passing of a day. Like watching a small lantern try to light up an entire room, with only the faint presence of light making its way out to the walls, so was England on this day. Elizabeth lay in her bed clutching her hands to her chest, holding on tightly to a silk ribbon tied around her neck. She knew that soon enough her light would flicker for the last time.

Elizabeth thought back upon her life and all of the twists and turns that had brought her to where she was today.

Her tiny fingers clutched tightly around the medallion that had hung around her neck, like they had done every night for the past fifteen years. She had memorized every groove and indentation of her creation. Sleepless nights had bothered Elizabeth over the previous number of years, and her attention would almost always focus on the medallion, and what it represented to her. Her fingers would run over the surface of the medallion, her version of counting sheep.

Her memories escaped back to her childhood, and her grandfather, the powerful King Edward I of England. She remembered vividly his powerful and forceful nature and the secrets that her mother said that he had kept.

Elizabeth had been nine years old when she saw it. Her mother Joan had taken Elizabeth and her brother and sisters to Windsor Castle to visit Elizabeth's grandfather, King Edward I of England, and his new wife for Christmas.

It was late one night, and Elizabeth couldn't sleep. The newness of the surroundings had been unsettling, and she tossed and turned for over an hour, before realizing that everyone else had gone to sleep. She quietly slipped out of the bed that she had shared with her older sister Eleanor. Unable to sleep, why not go exploring, she thought.

She lit the candle that was sitting next to the bed and cracked the door open and slid out into the long cold hallway that extended to the right and to the left for what seemed for miles. She knew the way through the castle to the central tower, although during the daytime she was never allowed to go into it. Now was her chance, she thought.

Her feet were cool as the cold stone floors penetrated her thin socks, and her pace quickened. Elizabeth hoped that running would warm up her body.

The stairway leading up into the tower came into sight and her pulse raced. Elizabeth knew that this was an area of the castle that had been off-limits to her and her siblings, and really anyone else, for that matter, that she knew about.

The spiral staircase was narrow, but to Elizabeth it seemed to be enormous. But everything to a six year old seems to be larger than life. She held the candlestick holder in front of her as she moved up the stairs one by one, with the light bending around each corner slightly in front of her.

Elizabeth looked up trying to determine how far up her journey might take her, and then she spotted it. She stopped and looked up, *seeing that it was completely out of place, and as she moved higher in the staircase it disappeared from her view.*

It was a door. A door built into the tower that Elizabeth was circling as she rose higher and higher. But it was only noticeable from below, completely hidden from the average climber of the stair when on the same level with the door.

As Elizabeth reached the height in the staircase approximately where she thought the door was located, she stopped and wondered how to work around the stone wall back to where the door was located.

Was there anything behind it? Was it just for show?

Elizabeth noticed stones that stuck out about a foot from the wall, with a pattern of about every other stone, creating a stepping-stone look that she believed would take her directly to the front of the door. She also had noticed that one false step and her body would fall ten to twenty feet down onto a stone stairwell.

Her tiny fingers on her left hand dug into the grooves created by the missing mortar between the two stones, while her right hand clung to the candle. If she were to drop the only source of light that she had, it could be a disaster getting down in complete darkness.

With her stockings left behind in a pile on the stairs, Elizabeth took her first step, carefully moving her body across each stepping stone. With each step, the journey seemed to get easier, with Elizabeth's thin body taking up very little space on each stone, and each stone got bigger and bigger the closer to the door that she got.

Then she was standing right in front of it. It was a door, only much smaller than anything Elizabeth had seen before. It was about half the size of the doors that she had been used to around her castle. She grasped the door handle and turned it and it was locked. The skeleton keyhole stared back at her, looking at Elizabeth directly in the eye. She peered into the hole to an abyss of darkness. The candle was of no use. If she wanted to know what was in that room, she would need to figure out how to open the door.

Elizabeth thought about the box in her room and the grouping of keys that she had collected as she and her family would visit various castles and houses throughout the country. She wondered if she could make any of them fit.

Elizabeth closed the door to the tower and had taken only a few quick steps back to her room when she heard the noise of footsteps coming toward her.

"Child, what are you doing up this early?" came the voice of Matilda, one of the many housekeepers at Windsor.

"I couldn't sleep," Elizabeth replied.

"Well, if your mother knew you were up wandering the halls of the house on such a cold night, she would be beside herself," Matilda responded back with the tone of a mother hen.

"Yes, ma'am," Elizabeth sheepishly answered, then opened the door to her room seeing that Eleanor was still asleep.

The lock to the door turned, and the door opened with the fourth key Elizabeth had pulled from her string of keys. Her hand trembled as she turned the handle and pushed the door open wide enough to light up the room with the candle that she held in her hand.

The small room lit up, and Elizabeth pushed her head in with a bit of concern, not knowing what would be found behind the door of this small hidden room.

Her tiny feet took cautious steps into the circular room, and she held the candle high above her head to maximize the light that it produced.

Her eyes widened in amazement to what she saw as she pivoted on her toes, looking around the room at what lined the walls and sat on the desks. Her eyes focused on one particular section of the wall, and she walked closer to get a better view, pulling her arm straight in front of her.

Elizabeth's eyes strained in the darkness trying to make out the words, and then she crossed herself, stared for a moment, and then backed out of the room and quickly made her way back to the bed, with a still sleeping Eleanor resting peacefully.

Her eyes focused on the ceiling, and Elizabeth didn't sleep at all that night.

Chapter 27

The summer sun in Scotland seemed to remind me of a spring day in Boston, with a lot of rain and clouds and the sun peeking its head out on occasion. It wasn't exactly cold, but it wasn't very warm either. Our room was decorated with a simple twin bed, a dark-stained dresser and an older television, something I would have expected to have seen had I travelled back in time to the year 1982.

Gabriela and I stayed in the bed and decided to use this as our detective's desk. We would in essence lay out the scene of the crime and then put our problem solving skills to work and see what we could solve. Without a whole lot to go on we thought our chances had run their course. But we knew a few facts, and they told us a few things that were necessary to solve this case.

1. We had a poem that seemed to be written by someone with the initials EDCBA.

2. We had a medallion that also seemed to be a key, that when set on the poem in certain positions would reveal more clues.

But more than anything else, I realized that the greatest asset that we possessed during this entire process was each other. Gabriela's strengths seemed to be my weaknesses, and those things that Gabriela struggled with seemed to be where I stood out the most. We were making a pretty good couple, I thought to myself.

We had decided before we sat down to figure out this latest puzzle not to talk as we studied. We wanted two sets of fresh, unbiased eyes looking at this puzzle. We would give each other as much time as we needed to look at it and examine how this all fit together.

"Honey, did you mean what you said to me in the alley yesterday?" Gabriela asked me in a sweet and innocent tone.

"Do you mean when I told you that I loved you?" I replied back.

"Yes," she answered.

"Of course I did, and I do!" I answered back, and then leaned over the bed with the papers dividing us and gave Gabriela a kiss. She looked at me with a smile that lingered for what seemed like an hour.

We looked over the poem, taking turns using the medallion to try to decipher what the relationship was between the two items. It was a lot like pulling apart a new ready-to-assemble desk without the instructions. It all looks really great in theory, but without the instructions, we were screwed.

The poem had been written on parchment paper and was surprisingly clear considering the age of the document. The words were clean and not smudged at all, with only the occasional crease and/or fold in the paper's makeup. Someone had taken a lot of time and preparation to preserve this document.

"This is not making any sense!" I finally blurted out. "I cannot make any sense of this. My eyes are going crossed. I think that we need a key from a map or something."

Gabriela didn't respond, and remained focused on the paper. Her eyes were focused intently on the document, and then she looked up at me.

"I think you figured it out and have solved it," she replied.

"I haven't solved anything," I shot back.

"Look! Notice on the medallion. If you look closely you will see something. Do you see those small, seemingly insignificant letters on four opposite sides?" she said.

I reached for my reading glasses, wondering why I hadn't had them on the entire time we were looking at this.

"The four letters are N, S, E, W. I don't know why I hadn't noticed that before. And if you look here on the poem, there are four places where those same letters appear randomly on the paper," she announced.

"So you are thinking that we can just lay the medallion down on the paper and write the words that come through the stones?" I asked.

"I would think so, but I have never done this before," she replied back.

I took out a piece of paper and pen and began to write as Gabriela lined up the medallion on the paper with its coinciding letters. She started with the N, finding the North on both the poem and the medallion and putting them together, and then Gabriela started reading off words, or parts of words, that came through the almost clear stones. Then she moved to the S, and read of all the words and phrases, and then to the E, and then finally to the W.

We soon had a collage of words that didn't seem to make any sense, any sense at all. It felt as if we were playing a board game by putting words together to make a sentence. But in this game there were no cheat sheets in the back of a book, and there were no "tomorrow's newspapers" that provided the answers. We were working completely blind, and we knew that if we didn't have it correct, we would be heading in a completely different direction—the wrong direction.

I could hear the slight vibration of my phone, and I looked around trying to see where I had laid it down. I stood up from the bed and walked over to the table in our room, and found it eventually in a pair of jeans that I had changed out of the night before.

"Who is it?" Gabriela asked.

"It is Lilly. She wants to know if we have taken anymore pictures for her, and she also wants to know when I will be home," I replied back with my voice trailing off.

The room got quiet as we both realized that sooner or later, this, whatever it was between us, was going to end. Maybe on a temporary basis, but it still was going to end. At some point in the near future we would both be getting on opposite planes heading in opposite directions. The thought of that cut me to the core, but I knew that was the way it had to be. I thought about Gabriela and what could happen to her with Marco lurking. What was he capable of doing to her? What, if anything, was there that I could do for her?

After reading the text from Lilly, I saw my phone flashing the email inbox icon indicating that I had other emails and texts that I hadn't seen, including one from my friend Dr. Bowles.

"Hey beautiful, listen to this," I said with a tone of excitement in my voice.

"What's that?" she replied.

"It's an email from Dr. Bowles," I said.

"Jonah. I hope this email finds you well. I did a little looking on your initialized signature, and I think I might have an answer for you. It seems there was a woman who lived in the early 1300s named Elizabeth de Clare. She was married a few times, and from my sources, she could have possibly created her initials as Elizabeth De Clare Burgh Amory. All names from marriages. She was the money behind Clare College at the University of Cambridge. Kind of a fascinating woman. Hope this helps. How is that beautiful woman you were with? Take care. Russ."

"You told him that I was beautiful?" Gabriela asked.

"Well, I certainly couldn't lie to him," I responded.

I remembered something, something I had already known before this from my previous life in relationships, but that was reinforced at this moment. Even on this eve of the discovery of a poem hopefully to be solved, with a clue that seemed to have now been unwrapped, the most important thing in Gabriela's mind was that fact that I had told someone that she was beautiful. I smiled at her, and then I paused and took all of her in at that moment. She was more than beautiful to me. She was everything.

"You are more than beautiful," I whispered in her ear. Then I kissed her.

I pulled up a search engine on my laptop and searched for the name of Elizabeth de Clare Burgh Amory. I found a link on a medieval England nobility Web site and started to read out loud.

"Elizabeth de Clare was born in 1295, to her parents, Gilbert de Clare, one of the wealthiest and most powerful men in England, and Joan of Acre, the daughter of King Edward I of England. After the deaths of both of her parents, Elizabeth, at the age of thirteen, was sent with her brother to Ireland, in an arrangement to marry siblings."

"Within a couple of years, Elizabeth had given birth to her first and only son, and the next year her husband was killed in battle. The following year, in 1314, Elizabeth's only brother was also killed in battle, leaving no male heir to the massive inheritance that her brother had collected after his father's death, leaving his estate to be divided up among his three sisters, including Elizabeth."

"Elizabeth's uncle, now King Edward II, saw this sudden transfer of wealth and Elizabeth being single as a way to control her fortune. Edward called Elizabeth back to England, forcing her to leave her son behind, with every intention of having Elizabeth marry one of Edward's supporters."

"The plan backfired. As Elizabeth waited at Bristol Castle for her next marriage in England, she was abducted by Theobald II of Ireland, and was taken back to Ireland so that they could get married instead. Some believe that they had been engaged before Elizabeth was brought back to England."

"Six months into the marriage, Theobald was dead and Elizabeth was pregnant now and caring for the three daughters from Theobald's previous marriage. Once again, her uncle had Elizabeth brought back to England, to marry one of Edward's supporters."

"At the age of twenty-one, Elizabeth gave birth to her second child, a daughter, and a few weeks later Elizabeth was married to Sir Roger D'Amory. Within five years Roger was dead, and after much political upheaval Elizabeth finally had her estate restored under the reign of her nephew, King Edward III."

"After Roger's death Elizabeth took a vow of chastity, taking herself off the aristocratic marriage market, and spent the remainder of her life helping others, giving to those less fortunate, and funding Clare College at the University of Cambridge until her death in 1360, almost forty years after the death of her last husband."

I looked up at Gabriela, and looking back at me she said without hesitation, "We are going to Clare College."

Chapter 28

Gabriela and I went out for dinner, trying to find something in Edinburgh that we hadn't yet experienced on our trip. There were restaurants that served the traditional haggis, fish and chips, and burgers and steaks. We decided to stop in at a place called Wallace's Revenge, kind of a hole-in-the-wall place that had its front door off of the main street down an alley.

I looked at Gabriela as we walked in and raised my shoulders and eyebrows wondering what Molli, our hotel desk clerk, was talking about.

Wallace's Revenge was what we discovered to be the anti-English establishment. Everything, and I mean everything, in this place spoke of Scotland, and one of their traditions was that you had to order in Gaelic, and if you didn't speak it, you had better learn it in a hurry.

"A bheil a' Ghàidhlig agaibh?" I heard from behind my head, as our waitress, Heather, approached our table.

"Do you really speak Gaelic?" I asked.

"I do a little (*in gaelic*)," Gabriela replied.

"I told you that I know a thing or two about languages. Didn't I?" she continued.

"Well, yes...but Gaelic?" I shot back.

"Could we have just a few minutes?" Gabriela said to Heather.

"Sure. I will be back in a bit," Heather said as she walked back toward the kitchen.

"You never cease to amaze me," I said, taking a sip of ice water.

We both ordered an amazing burger and a side of fries that Molli had been completely right about, and then spent some time looking over the clues. Gabriela had gone into an office supply store and found some note cards that we could write all of the words and/or partial words on and try to put this little puzzle together.

Laid out on the table in front of us:

Look, Wall, His, Seek, H, Er, My, Face, On, England, Down, You, igh, F, M, T, Gh, M, Ro, Sod.

There were partial words that seemed to fit together more easily than the clue as a whole. We wondered what would happen if we put it together but it was incorrect. Then what? Fourteen words, with the main words to us being "England," "tower," and "wall."

There was just too much to go wrong if we put it together incorrectly. We could either be looking for a "sod tower down on high England," or "England face high on sod."

If Russ was correct, then the logical key to all of this was Elizabeth de Clare, and how did she connect to the clue? There was the word "my" in the clue, which we decided had to refer to her. The words "England," "tower," and "wall" seemed logical for a location that Elizabeth would be referring to. We needed to get to Cambridge and Clare College and find out more about Elizabeth.

The check came to our table, Gabriela said "thank you," and we walked out and found a taxi.

"Good evening to ya," the taxi driver said as we slid into the backseat. "Where can I take you this fine evening?"

"We are heading to the train station," I said as he pulled out into the street. "But we first need to head back to our hotel and grab our luggage. It's at the Edinburgh Suites on Center Street. Can you wait for us for a bit?"

"You two seem to be in a big hurry. Did you rob a bank or something? Need to get out of town fast?" Ian said with a chuckle.

"No, nothing like that, we are trying to catch a train tonight to Cambridge. It leaves in just under an hour," I replied back.

"I will get you there in no time," he assured us. "What are you two doing here in Scotland? On vacation?"

"You can say that. Something like that," Gabriela answered.

Gabriela and I boarded the train toward England with one destination in mind, Clare College, until I received a message on my phone.

Marco had been released from jail earlier in the evening. And I wasn't sure what, or if, I should tell Gabriela.

Chapter 29

The train ride south was a lot like our train ride north, only this time we were traveling down the east coast of England in the dark of the night. Distant lights only told me of the places that I was missing, and the places that I would not see with my own eyes during the day, at least not on this trip.

Gabriela had fallen asleep without knowing that Marco was out of jail, and who knows where he would be lurking next. I thought it best not tell her for now, and let her get as good a night's sleep as you can get while traveling by train. I remembered her reaction to me in the hotel in Salisbury, the portrait of fear painted in her face and body as she looked out over the parking lot from our hotel window knowing that he was out there somewhere. I remembered the tears that streamed down her face as she told me the story, the real story of Marco.

I could not let her go through that again, at least not tonight. I wanted her to just focus on whatever would be dancing in her head tonight, and we would tackle the Marco situation in the morning.

I wanted and needed to know more about Elizabeth. Where would we need to go once we arrived in Cambridge? What could we pull out of the unsolved puzzle that would help us make sense of anything? These were questions that I wanted to have as many answers to as possible before we arrived in the morning. So I got online and started to search more about Elizabeth.

I found out that after her last husband had died she had made a declaration of celibacy, while she was still in her late twenties. Quite a commitment for someone that young, who would spend the next forty years giving to the poor, helping the needy, starting a college, and, by all of our calculations, creating a treasure and all the clues that were needed to find it.

I continued reading and found that her mother was buried in the abbey near Clare College, and that many people believed that there were miracles that happened at that location. I found that Elizabeth had built a tower near the abbey and I assumed that would be the logical place for us to start looking once we arrived there. She had also planted and cared for a large rose garden next to the abbey. Something to do in your spare time, I thought.

A portrait of Elizabeth on the Web site showed a woman at peace with herself, and her life. Her left hand rested on her chest, with a book held in the other hand, almost as if clutching on to learning and signifying how close it was to her heart.

The constant clicking of the train running against the tracks had begun to put me in a state of near sleep. The cadence of the tracks and the motion of the train acted a lot like a pendulum used by a hypnotist—tick, tock, tick, tock—and I was beginning to fall asleep somewhere in the blackened countryside of Scotland.

Gabriela shifted in her sleep and I reached over and rubbed her back, trying to calm her and also trying to make sure she didn't wake up. Her attention needed to be with the images and thoughts in her brain and whatever it was that she dreamed about. I looked at her and wondered. I wanted her to be safe, and I worried about her and Marco. I will fly back to Boston and she will travel back to Italy, and then we will have to decide what is next for us.

Will we look back on the past number of days as a blessing in each of our lives, like the popular saying goes, "everyone comes into our lives for a reason and a season," or will we continue to see each other and see what happens next?

I knew the reason. I just didn't know how long the season. I thought back to Walter fitz Alan, being told that he could live in his new castle until he harvested his first crop, or his own growing season. He chose to plant oak, those oak sprouts that still have firm roots to this day. Maybe Gabriela and I could choose a much longer season. I just had no idea how to make it all work on two continents. But now that I thought about it, Walter improvised from the moment his men arrived back at the castle. And so I should with Gabriela.

My eyes began to shut and I fought hard to keep them open. I don't know why I didn't want to sleep, but there was something about this train that was making me uneasy.

I picked up Gabriela's legs from lying across mine, and I stood up, deciding to take a walk down the train to see if I could find something to drink. The door closed and I walked down the long corridor to find a food compartment, or a vending machine.....or something.

It was midnight, and all of the services were shut down for the night. I found a vending machine and purchased a Mountain Dew, something I hadn't tasted for almost two weeks. Why I thought I needed caffeine at midnight was beyond me.

The train began to slow down, having just crossed over the border into England at Berwick, and I decided to get off and get some air. Maybe there was something to eat at the train station.

The train began its slow departure from the nearly empty train station, and I walked back to our compartment with some fruit and an assortment of drinks, wishing like anything to have a great slice of pizza. Something else I was noticing about Gabriela: she was "helping" me eat right.

I watched out the windows as the train picked up momentum leaving the station and found it odd that someone was running with the train. The scene looked a lot like some movie, where there is some guy trying to find the love of his life as she leaves town heading to college, or the cop trying to track down the bad guy.

I paused for a moment, and watched closely as he lost momentum and couldn't keep up. I adjusted my eyes again. If I didn't know any better, I would have sworn it was Marco.

Chapter 30

Cambridge, England, was everything I thought it would be, with the exception of our arriving after a sleepless night on a train, and one that I thought for sure Marco knew we were on.

There were beautiful cathedrals with high arches and unsurpassed architecture, according to Gabriela. But was Marco hiding behind their walls waiting for us?

There were quaint houses and the River Cam running through the town, but was Marco watching us from a car, waiting for the moment to attack? I looked at the village square and loved the summer morning, watching people feeding the pigeons, and others at play. Would Marco expose his ugliness to everyone in public? I hadn't thought so.

I thought that after he had followed us for as long as he had, watching our every move, knowing that I was with Gabriela, that maybe he would wait for the perfect time to get her alone. But after he barged the door at the hotel in Glastonbury, knowing that I could be with her, I realized that he wasn't afraid of anything—of anyone.

"Honey, where are we going first?" Gabriela asked me.

"I think there are a few things that we need to talk about first," I replied back.

"OK, what is it?" she asked.

"I got an email late last night," I started.

She looked puzzled, like maybe it was from my friend Russ. "And he said?" she asked.

"Who?" I shot back.

"Russ. What did he have to say about the puzzle?" she replied.

"The email wasn't from Russ. It was from the Glastonbury police department." My voice began to trail off. "Marco was released yesterday," I added.

"What?" she said with a voice of exasperation.

"He was able to post bond," I answered back. "But there is something else." Gabriela looked at me with a quizzical look. "I think I saw him running with the train when we left Berwick last night. I can't be sure, but it certainly looked a lot like him."

"Was he on the train?" she asked.

"No. He was trying to run and catch up with it. But I get the sense that he knew we were on that train," I explained. "If it was him at all. I don't know."

We sat in silence and once again Gabriela went off to her place, deep in thought like she was a million miles away, or at least nine hundred miles, to a time and a place that she wanted to forget entirely. But Marco wouldn't let her.

I reached over to hold her hand and it was cold, not only the reception that I got from her, but her skin actually felt cold.

"Hey Gabriela, I don't know. Maybe it wasn't him at all. Maybe it was just my imagination playing tricks on me, since I had just read that he had been released," I tried to explain.

She continued to sit in silence, staring off into the distance, and I wondered if I should just let her deal with this newly found information on her own, or if I should be more proactive and help her take her mind off of things. She reminded me of the Cameron Frye character from *Ferris Bueller's Day Off*. How he went into a trance when he realized that the miles on his father's 1961 Ferrari 250 GT California Spyder could not be reversed. Gabriela was in a trance.

"Can we go for a walk?" I asked. "I have some great ideas as to where we might be able to find some clues about Elizabeth."

Gabriela stood up like a zombie, and we began walking toward Clare College, and Elizabeth de Clare, I hoped. The summer sun was warm and a breeze filtered through the streets and alleyways. I reached over to hold her hand as we walked and I could feel the coolness starting to go away.

We crossed the picturesque River Cam and I wanted to stop and take some pictures of the beautiful river with the green grass that was immaculately cared for and the stone walking bridge. But I realized that finding Elizabeth was a lot like our train ride here overnight. The river pictures would have to wait for another day. Right now we were on a quest; a quest for answers, and our time was running out. Not just for my time in England, but I also thought that we needed to move as quickly as possible, and try to put some distance between us and Marco, if in fact Marco was following us at all.

We walked now as two people with somewhere to go, in a hurry, and I wondered if this new information wouldn't change our relationship forever.

Clare College came into view and I looked for the tower, the tower that Elizabeth had constructed. I glanced to my left and right, not seeing anything. We needed to find it so that we could see what our next step was. We approached an information booth and found a series of visitor guides, and I looked for one with a map that might take us to Elizabeth's tower.

Gabriela stopped walking and pulled my hand toward her, wrapping her arms around me, and I could feel her body begin to shake against mine. Her tears began to flow again, and I just stood there for a moment, what seemed like an eternity, wanting to say something, but realizing that there are moments in our lives when the best thing said is nothing at all. This was one of those moments.

Gabriela released her grasp of me, and I wiped her eyes as she looked up at me and I kissed her. Nothing was said to me about Marco, and she clutched my hand and I could feel its warmth again.

"What are we looking for?" she asked.

"We are looking for Elizabeth's tower," I said, looking at the map that I pulled out in front of both of us. "But I am not seeing anything on this map that looks like a tower or anything like that."

"Maybe there is someone here who can help us find it," Gabriela replied, and then looked off for someone to talk to.

"Excuse me. Could you answer a question for us?" she asked what looked to be a student, in his mid-twenties, wearing a black bow tie and a mostly red, plaid, short-sleeve shirt.

"I will if I can," he replied.

"We are looking for a tower that is located by a rose garden. Do you know where anything like that is?" she asked.

"Oh, the Clare roses? It is about a twenty minute walk in that direction," he said, pointing to the east. "There is a building next to it with a tower of sorts, but I don't know if it is exactly a tower."

"Thank you so much," I added.

The tower finally came into view, and as we approached it the fragrance of the Clare roses overtook both of us. We peeked through the walled area and were amazed at the uniqueness of this place. I thought back to the beauty of the Cadzow Oaks, planted only a few years before this garden, and the stark contrast that they were to each other. *Inside the old, grows the new,* I thought.

The red brick walls were old, but I noticed that there were changes that had taken place, with various pieces of the wall changed to make viewing the roses much more easy from outside the wall.

I tightened my grip around Gabriela's hand and we walked toward the bell tower building with no expectations, but with a sincere hope that we were heading in the right direction. As we entered the building a sign next to the door read:

The Elizabeth de Clare House for the Weary and Poor in all of us.

Come and rest your souls and be renewed and refreshed.

We looked at each other and opened the doors, and I think we both felt like if there was anyone who needed to be renewed and refreshed, we did. The large open room was filled with small rounded tables and chairs, and a wall of books to the right. We saw an assortment of people using the "library," from elderly couples, students, and those who just needed a cool place to sit and rest.

We approached the information desk, and an older woman in her seventies dressed in a herringbone skirt and jacket, with her silver hair pulled back into a tight bun on the back of her head, smiled at us as we approached.

"Can I help you find something?" she asked.

"We wanted to know if you could tell us about this place. Its history and what it is used for," I asked.

"Well," she continued, pointing to a large painting on the wall directly behind her. "Elizabeth de Clare is the patron of this building and its surrounding areas. She had used this as her place of escape to think and ponder about things of importance to her. Originally this hallway was used to feed the poor and was used also as a place of worship, and anything else that was needed. Back in the 1340s it was also used as a place to bring those suffering from the bubonic plague, or Black Death, as they call it."

"Do you know what the tower was used for?" I asked.

"The tower bell was used originally to signal that service was about to begin, or that the food was ready for those that needed to come and partake," she answered. "I would imagine that it was used for a number of things. I do know that Elizabeth was the only person who used the tower for many years. If she were to be out of town, they would pull a bell out from an adjacent room and ring from the ground floor."

"Is there any way that we could go look down from the tower? I have recently become a huge fan of Elizabeth's and I would like to see things from the perspective that she had," I asked.

"A fan?" she questioned.

"Well." I struggled with the right wording. "Maybe the word that I am looking for is "admirer." I smiled.

She smiled back. "I understand completely. I have been an admirer of hers for nearly fifty years," she responded with an identical smile. "We normally don't allow visitors to go to the bell tower without a chaperon, but I think in this case we can make an exception."

I looked back up at the portrait of Elizabeth, admiring the artist that had painted her likeness. Then as I took a closer look, I noticed something about the painting that I hadn't at first glance.

She was wearing a medallion. I looked at Gabriela, and I shifted my eyes toward the painting. She grabbed my hand firmly and we followed Eleanor to the door that led up the stairs to the tower.

The door shut tightly behind us and we started our assent up each stone step, and Gabriela looked at me.

"I am starting to wonder about you," she said. "I would have thought that you would have known that every woman checks out the jewelry of any other woman they see, in a painting or not."

Chapter 31

We arrived in the top of the tower with an expectation of no expectations. The circular area was about twelve feet across, with a smooth stone floor and a stone wall that rose about four feet. The view from above was spectacular, and I looked down to the rose garden and wondered what it must have been like for Elizabeth to sit here and look down on her creation, once finished.

The entire view was breathtaking as Gabriela and I looked around at the surrounding lands that made up this place of renewing one's soul. I was beginning to see why.

"There has got to be a clue up here somewhere. Hasn't there?" I said. I began to look around at the stone wall that surrounded us for a clue or something that even resembled a clue. The bell hung above our heads with the clapper having been removed. I looked up into the brick arch above it and couldn't figure out if we were even in the right spot.

The sound of quiet footsteps was heard coming up the staircase, and I turned to see the lady who had helped us at the information desk.

"I didn't properly introduce myself. My name is Maude De Brose. I am Elizabeth De Clare's twelfth great-granddaughter. Are you looking for something specific?" she asked in a very kind way.

I looked at Gabriela and she smiled back.

"This might sound like a crazy idea, but we believe that Elizabeth hid something. A treasure, if you will. We have been following clues for days, and the last clue brought us here. We don't even know if we are on the right track," I told her.

Maude paused for a moment, and then she spoke.

"I feel like I have been waiting for you two my entire life," she said, clasping her hands in front of her face. Then she continued. "When I was a young girl, my mother ran this facility much like I do now. I would spend hours in an office reading, and I would often climb up into the attic and look for things; I would explore. One summer day, not too much unlike this one, I climbed up into the attic, and I opened up a trunk that contained a lot of books and documents. One specific book caught my attention. It was a larger journal, with very frail pages, and even as a twelve year old, I knew the importance of them and how delicate they would be. I began reading this journal, which I found out was the journal of Elizabeth herself."

"I read every word in this journal over and over. Elizabeth spoke of the things that she did daily, the people that came to this building to be fed, and the life that she lived until her death."

"There was one entry toward the end of the journal that said, 'Someday they will come, and I hope that they arrive, with love, forgiveness, and compassion.'

"I never knew what she meant by that. Then in 1986, the tower covering the bell needed some work done to it, and the workers found a leather satchel that had been sealed inside of the inner wall. They brought it to me and I read all of the contents. Suddenly, the phrase she wrote in the journal made more sense."

"'Someday they will come, and I hope that they arrive, with love, forgiveness and compassion.'"

Gabriela inserted, "I don't think I understand. What does that have to do with us?"

Maude opened up the leather satchel that she held firmly in her hands, pulling out a sheet of paper from one of its pockets. The paper had been inserted in a clear protective sleeve.

"I didn't know what else to do with it. I thought that if I gave it to just anyone, whatever is on this paper could have fallen into the wrong hands. I thought it was best to just protect it the best way that I could and then wait, hoping that someone, someday, would come here looking for it."

"Can I see it?" I asked.

"Yes. I do believe that it belongs to you," she replied.

Gabriela and I glanced at each other, then looked back at Maude with puzzlement.

"I just know. You are the ones who need to see this, and read its contents," she replied back.

With that, Maude turned and started her descent back toward the door at the bottom of the stairs.

"This stuff has just got to stop happening to us," I said.

"Why? Where would we be if it didn't?" Gabriela replied.

We pulled the paper close to us, and we started to read.

Chapter 32

The Son of God is a glorious sight, that awakens your senses within,

When you look deep inside, your soul opens up, making the veil quite thin.

Our eyes were meant to Look toward God, with all that we do and say.

Our mouths were made to partake of his fruit, savoring each bite each day.

Our Ears open up hearing his words, in music and voice grow like a seed.

Our hands touch those who need our help, to bless and heal and feed.

Our noses smell goodness in all of the creations that God has put here to see,

But your quest to find his face is in the sense that begins to awaken in spring.

Look around you now, and I hope that you see all the senses that surround you are near,

But you will need the help from the Arimathea bush, now it should become very clear.

His Son brought Sight, Sound, Taste, Touch and Smell reminding of all things his way.

The Five Righteous Senses are given by God, and we must seek his forgiveness each day.

Chapter 33

Gabriela and I looked around the grounds from on top of this bell tower and tried to take in all of the things that were within the poem. The grounds that surrounded us were filled with various things. First there was the rose garden, and off in another direction was a building that, Gabriela told me, was an old kitchen. I would assume the building was placed there to keep the heat away from the main building.

There was a statue of Jesus touching a blind man, allowing him to see, and another building that looked like a small church, which we had heard an organ playing from when we had first arrived.

There was a small reflection pond that on a clear calm day could serve as a mirror, but I thought about all of these things and what they might mean to us.

"It is really quite simple," said Gabriela as she walked around the circular lookout. "They are all here. Touch," pointing to the statue of Jesus healing. "Taste," pointing toward the kitchen. "Hearing," motioning toward the church. "Sight," the reflection pond. "And finally..."

"Smell," I said. "It's in the rose garden. The poem mentions the Arimathea bush, and it is all becoming clear." Then I pulled out the clear stone medallion from the bag.

"I think we need to go start smelling the roses," Gabriela said.

We shut the door quietly behind us, smiled at Maude and exited the building as she smiled back.

The wrought iron gate that led into the rose garden seemed to have been created centuries ago. And as we walked in, my mind took me back to a time that hardly anyone knew. I thought about this lady, Elizabeth de Clare, and the time and effort and struggle it must have been for her to create such a series of clues. I thought of the value of whatever it was that she had in her possession, and how important it was for her to protect it to this extent.

We walked around the rose garden grounds and we both admired the thought and effort that went into its creation. The beds were cut with precision and manicured to perfection. I thought back to my own youth and the stories of my own great-grandfather living in England, and the stories my grandmother would tell of his immaculate garden. It must be something English, I thought, and about keeping sacred things sacred.

We walked to the center of the garden, where a large circular sitting area had taken up the center of this large flower. It was made up of stone masonry and had a sitting bench built in all the way around. I was looking for clues, any kind of clues. This really was the worst part of this trip; it was looking at England through a straw. In my history, I had loved to look at things with a big perspective, the whole picture. But I was now only allowed to look at small specific things. I could only imagine how Gabriela was doing with her work here being put on hold.

A brass ring was set into the top of the circular seating area that was about ten inches wide. There were designs of circles, diamonds that made up most of the interior of the brass, with words and letters making up more of the design.

Gabriela ran her fingers over the brass trying to figure out what could lead us to the answer.

"What are you thinking?" she asked.

"I am thinking that this whole process is starting to take its toll," I answered with a bit of frustration in my voice.

"Where is the medallion?" she asked.

"Which one? We are starting to get quite a collection!" I shot back.

"The clear one," she said with a calmness that had always impressed me about her.

I handed Gabriela the medallion, and memories shot back to that night in Glastonbury and kneeling down in the water looking up into its mouth, and now here we were feeling like we were on the verge of finding whatever it was that had eluded us to this point.

"I think we will find that the clear medallion will be the key for us to solve this little mystery," she said with the confidence of the architecturologist that I had fallen in love with. "Let me show you what I mean."

"On our medallion," she said, pointing to the directional letters, "there are North, South, East and West. If you look on the brass ring here, you will find circle designs at the points of North, South, East and West, with each having our directional letters in the design. The circles also are the same size of the medallion."

"I believe," Gabriela said, placing the medallion in the circle labeled North, with the medallion "N" matching up with the "N" in the circle, "that if we lay it down right there, we should get some answers?"

I stepped forward and put on my reading glasses, trying to use anything to help with the sunshine that was now bright, high in the sky. I leaned forward and looked down at the stones to see what it was that they might reveal.

"'He lays' is all that is says," I said to Gabriela as I looked up at her.

"Well, let's move to the next circle. Do you think it would be clockwise, counter-clockwise, or N, S, E, W?" she asked.

"I think we should go clockwise to start," I answered back.

Gabriela laid the medallion on the EAST circle. I peered closely, looking for what might be there for us to find.

"It looks like it says, 'WITH ACRE,'" I read aloud.

"He lays with Acre?" she asked back.

"Let's check the rest of them," I replied.

We moved down to the SOUTH circle, and I looked in again.

"The SON," I read.

"And the WEST circle?" Gabriela asked.

The medallion was placed in the final circle. And I knew that we should be getting close to finalizing this chapter of our story.

I remembered the day I saw Gabriela, as I stood in the kitchen of the Coalchesters' with my hair disheveled, and I saw her head over the top of the newspaper that she was reading. I could have not imagined then, to see us here now, working so well together in unison as we had woven our way through the various issues that had been laid before us. I had fallen in love with Gabriela, and I realized that regardless of what happened next, I should capture each moment with her in my heart for now, cherishing it, and savoring it. There would be days, whether we found our ways together past this point or not, that I would miss her. Today's memories would give me a smile, an inner peace, and memories to go back to during tomorrow's times of disappointment and missing her.

"Before we look at the last circle," I said, taking her hand and pulling her into me, "I love you. I want you to know that you have become the best part of my life. This time with you....I wouldn't have changed a thing. With whatever is happening next, or with whatever direction we go, I want you to know. I love you."

Gabriela wrapped her arms around me tightly, saying nothing. I kissed her forehead, and then she picked up the medallion and placed it in the WEST circle. She leaned forward and read.

"IS FOUND," she said.

"He Lays With Acre The Son Is Found," I repeated back.

"I am completely confused," Gabriela said back to me. "An acre is an area of land. What does that mean?"

"This is where I can come in and help. King Edward I, before he was king, was in the Holy Land during The Crusades. His pregnant wife gave birth to a daughter, and then they were called back to England at the news of his father's death, making him the new King of England. Their daughter was named Joan of Acre, with Acre being one of the only places in the Middle East during The Crusades that the Christians never lost a hold of."

"Joan of Acre came home, and eventually married Gilbert de Clare, making her the mother of…"

"Elizabeth de Clare," Gabriela finished.

"We need to find out where Joan of Acre is buried," I inserted.

We hurried back to the train station, with our luggage secured in a locker there. I left Gabriela to find something for us to eat, and I went to find a rental car. Clare, where Joan of Acre was buried, was only twenty miles away, and with no other options a car seemed to be the most feasible way to travel.

I found a car lot and at this point anything would do. Cars had never been a big thing for me. As long as they drove well, were maintained, and looked respectable, I really didn't care. At this point, we could have rented a horse and buggy and I would have been quite fine with it.

I pulled back into the train station lot and Gabriela was waiting with a couple of sandwiches. I was starving.

"Nice car," she said, making a bit of fun with the MG that I had found on the lot. "I love it."

"I didn't care about anything, as long as it would get us to Clare," I replied, and took a bite of my tuna sandwich.

Chapter 34

We pulled into the small village of Clare, with no idea of what do next. There was a small market store that looked a lot like the small grocery store that had been in the small town that I had grown up in in the Pacific Northwest—a place that sold everything.

There were hanging plants for sale on the outside awning, and bags of planting soil, pots, and flowers, all for sale. This had to have been the only place to buy anything around there, with the exception of driving into Cambridge. This was exactly like a place that I grew up in.

We entered the store, and the bell rang that was mounted on the inside of the wall above the door. A very plump lady wearing a lime green dress and white floral apron greeted us at the door, and looked at us like we were a gold mine.

"Good afternoon to ya, folks. I haven't seen you in here before," she said with a voice that seemed to be high enough that maybe at times only dogs would hear her.

"Good afternoon to you, as well. Could you help us with directions?" I asked. Gabriela and I had noticed that each time help was needed, if it was a man we were asking for help it was best if she was the one to talk and ask questions, and vice-versa.

"Well, of course," she answered. "Is there anything that I can get you while we talk? A ice cold lemonade? How about a pint of Ale? We also have a wide assortment of maps, and gift mugs."

"Lemonade sounds lovely. Anything for you, honey?" I asked as I turned to Gabriela and smiled.

"Lemonade sounds perfect," she replied.

Millie, the store owner, proceeded to pull two cans of lemonade out of the cooler section, and opened them both up for us, and then proceeded to ring them up on the register.

"That'll be two pounds fifty," she said with a smile.

Feeling like we had just been robbed, I smiled back.

"Can you tell us how to get to the abbey?" I asked.

"Why, I sure can. It is just about five blocks down this road. You really can't miss it," she replied.

We got into our car and headed in the direction that she put us in, and I thought again about all of the missed photo opportunities in this perfect little town. If we could just get through today; maybe tomorrow.

We pulled into a small parking lot and stood up, getting out of the car with a "here we are again" look that we gave each other, feeling like we were salesman going into yet one more meeting.

The abbey was old, and seemed to be in a state of ruin, but currently in use. The landscape wasn't as cared for as we had experienced everywhere else in England, but especially at the Clare roses. There were dead vines that had once crawled over the wall only to find death, and the word "disheveled" seemed to be the best word to describe it. This didn't seem fitting for a place to lay a princess to rest. But we walked toward the building anyway.

No one seemed to be around, so Gabriela and I walked around the grounds looking for some headstones, or any sign of the burial place of Joan of Acre.

As we rounded a corner toward the back of the grounds, a sign was seen on the wall of the back of the building. As we walked closer it read:

Here in 1307 was buried Joan of Acre, Countess of Glouchester,

daughter of Edward I and Eleanor of Castile

"It doesn't seem very fitting of royalty, don't you think?" Gabriela asked.

"Not at all," I replied.

We found what seemed to be the stone covering of her burial spot. But the clue that we had brought with us seemed to state that we were needing to look close to Joan.

"The Son, He Lays, with Acre, is found," I repeated. "It has to be somewhere near her tomb."

We began combing through the tall uncut grass, parting it and looking deep toward the roots for any sign of anything.

"I think I found something," Gabriela said with a voice of excitement.

I moved over to Gabriela, kneeling in the grass. She had found a small headstone that was flat in the ground, covered with dirt, dead grass, and was hidden from the naked eye by overgrown grass. We began to clear away the stone, which had a face that was about one foot by two feet. The first thing that came into view was a Star of David on one half, and Gabriela continued to brush away the debris from the other half of the headstone.

"Look at this. There is a carved out circle in the stone," Gabriela said while fishing out the dirt and waste that had sat buried in the hole for who knows how long. She found a small stick and began digging out the dirt from the stone.

"Can you get me a bottle of water out of my purse?" she asked

The hole in the stone was filled with water, which turned most of the dirt into a sloppy mud. I took a towel and wiped it clean until the entire carved out section seemed to fully reveal itself.

"Do you see what I see?" Gabriela asked.

"Yes, I do," I replied.

I pulled open the bag that I had thrown over my shoulder with most of our supplies in it, and pulled out the first medallion that I had found at Battle. The carved hole in the rock had been carved out to fit the medallion perfectly in its grooves. It fit like a glove.

"Aren't you supposed to press something now, and have some secret door open up?" Gabriela asked.

"I wish it were that simple," I answered, pushing anything that resembled a button, or a key to a secret passageway, wondering why Indiana Jones had it so easy. I chuckled.

"I think that whatever we are supposed to find is buried in this place, underneath this grass. Why don't we come back tonight when it isn't so obvious? Besides that, I think we need a shovel, and I am not going back to that store here. We need to go back to Cambridge."

Chapter 35

The sun began to set on Clare as we drove back into the little village with a shovel and flashlight, having spent a few hours in a hotel room, catching up on all the important things of life—showering, brushing teeth, and more than anything...taking some time to relax and stretch out on a regular bed.

There was a certain amount of anticipation that had been building since we left Clare earlier in the day. It felt like this was the end for this little mystery. Whatever happened tonight would wrap this up once and for all.

The small village lay quiet in the warmth of summer. I was so used to seeing kids out playing baseball or basketball on a summer night. Here in England, it was soccer, with a group of kids playing off in a field as we drove into town.

We pulled into the parking lot for the abbey and looked at each other, as if to say, "Let's do this."

"We should have brought a metal detector?" I said out loud.

"Well, we are too late for that!" Gabriela replied.

I took the shovel and began to cut a rectangular area of grass where we thought that the contents might lay, about four feet by three feet. Once that was cut I rolled the grass back, trying to keep it all in one piece so that it would be easy to lay back into place once we were finished.

With the grass back, I began digging, and I looked at Gabriela and said, "Do you realize we are standing in an ancient English cemetery digging up what looks to be a grave of a child? How morbid is this?"

Gabriela laughed. "I am just standing here watching. You are the digger."

"If we get caught, can't you pull out some kind of Ancient Roman Archeology press pass or something?" I asked.

Just then I struck something with my shovel. I couldn't tell if it was a rock or something else, but it at least gave me hope that we were getting close. I dug, only now faster, trying to unearth whatever it was that I had struck with my shovel. Each shovel of dirt only added to the excitement. I finally found what seemed to be the outline of the box, buried about two feet under the surface.

It measured about three feet by two feet, and seemed like a very simple wooden box. But if this was what we thought that is was, it was a six to seven-hundred-year-old box. Gabriela and I got down on our knees and dug around the edges of it, trying to find a place that we could grab a hold of and pull it out.

Finally the time was here, and with all of our strength we pulled the box up out of the ground and placed it in the grass. We looked at each other with amazement, not really sure we could believe that we had actually gotten this far.

"There is a lock on the hinge," Gabriela said.

"It's quite rusty. Maybe we can just break the lock," I replied.

With a couple whacks with the shovel, the lock broke and fell, disappearing into the long grass. We both grabbed the wooden lid and picked it up together, to find a very ornate box that looked more like a pirate's chest, or something to store valuables in. Its lid was held firmly in place with two leather straps that wrapped around the box, with buckles to keep them from opening up.

I picked it up and carried it to the grass, thinking that maybe we should just take it to the car. We decided to stay there and open it up. The hole in the grass would be too noticeable.

The latches of the dark cherry wood trunk were beautiful. Gabriela started to unhook the buckles. Finally releasing the second latch, her hands were shaking. I reached over and placed my hands over hers, and leaned over and kissed her.

"Thank you," I said.

"Thank you for what?" she replied.

"That first day when we talked in that parking lot and I asked you to come with me. I couldn't have done this without you." And I kissed her again.

"I wouldn't have missed this for the world," she replied.

"Are you ready? On the count of three," I said.

"One, two, three," we said in unison, and then lifted up the lid the same way.

The trunk contained a number of artifacts. But we both just sat in silence looking at what we had finally found. There was a pair of leather sandals, a folded up piece of once white but now yellowing fabric, a lock of hair, and two scrolls, with one being about two feet wide, and the other less than a foot wide.

Gabriela picked up the fabric and the lock of hair and placed it in the lid of the trunk. I picked up the larger of the two scrolls and we both pulled the document out that was hidden from within it, and as we pulled, the enormity of what we had discovered hit us both.

It was a painting of a humble man sitting who wore a white robe. He was also wearing the sandals that sat in the trunk, and the color of his hair matched the lock of hair, as well.

"It is him, Our Lord and Savior," she said, with the tears starting to well up in her eyes.

I recognized once we pulled the entire document out that it was a painting of Jesus Christ. I wasn't sure how I knew that, but I did. I peered in amazement as we looked over the painting and at the detail that it contained. It looked nothing like those paintings from da Vinci, or Rembrandt, but looking very humble, with eyes that seemed to pierce your soul.

"Let's put this back in the scroll," I said. "At least until we have gotten back to our hotel."

"OK," she replied, wiping the tears from her eyes.

I grabbed the final scroll and pulled out the document that had been hidden for all these years. It was a handwritten document.

"Do you know what language this is?" I asked Gabriela.

"It is Greek," she answered, and then began to read.

My Righteous King Abgar,

Thou doest believe that the Son of God hath the power to heal thy afflictions? Doest thou believe that the time will come when all of thy infirmities will be washed away from thy mortal body? Be still my son, and know that I am God. Be of good faith, and as you read my words, know that I am the only way for you to become truly clean in both body and spirit.

It is not by the touch nor is it by the repetition of things which makes a man whole, but it is by his faith and his works that a man is made clean. Have faith my faithful servant, and know that even though I am not there, the Spirit is within you. Hold this letter in thy hands, reading word for word in faith, and your sins will be washed away; your afflictions will be remembered no more.

Your humble servant,

Jesus of Nazareth

The tears continued to stream down Gabriela's face as she put the letter back in its scroll.

"Do you realize that we have found quite possibly the greatest discovery in the history of Christianity?" I asked.

Gabriela looked at me like I was a little boy glad to hear that Aunt Ruth had passed away, because I knew that I would be out of school for a few days. I hadn't quite gotten it. She recognized that we were in the presence of Jesus Christ, not just his artifacts.

We packed up the trunk with our newly found treasure, carefully placing everything back in its place, and I carried it to the car. The original wooden box was placed back in the ground, the dirt was shoveled back into place, and the turf was laid over the top, putting our puzzle back together again.

I looked at Gabriela and smiled, knowing that our journey was almost over. I didn't know quite what to say. So I stood there, letting sacred things remain sacred.

Suddenly there came a sound of triumphant trumpets coming from Gabriela's bag. She looked up at me.

"Buona sera, Gabriela," came a voice from around the corner. It was the voice of a man. It was Marco.

Chapter 36

"Marco, what are you doing here?" I asked with fear trembling from my voice.

"I am here to take you home," Marco replied while walking toward me slowly. "I don't understand what you are even doing with this guy."

"You are not taking me anywhere. We are over. Why don't you get that?" I repeated back.

"Babe, I am asking you one more time."

Marco took a couple steps toward me.

"Hey, she said that she doesn't want to go with you," Jonah blurted out.

"I don't remember asking for your opinion," Marco replied.

Just then Marco lunged at me. Our bodies collided, arms and legs crashing into each other.

The darkness had really begun to settle in. It was hard to tell who was who. I fell back to the soil; my head struck the ground and my face slid across the now dampened grass. I could taste blood in my mouth.

Suddenly everything was quiet with the faint sound of racing footsteps out in the parking lot against a gravel surface. I turned my body quickly and I saw a silhouette of Jonah standing facing the parking lot.

"Babe, are you ok?" I asked. There was no response.

Jonah dropped to his knees.

"Did he hit you?" I asked again. Still no response.

I managed to get to my knees and I scrambled crawling to Jonah and was kneeling in front of him. His hands grasped his chest above his heart.

"Are you ok?" I asked again.

I grabbed his hands.

"I...caaa." Jonah struggled to get anything out of his mouth.

I pulled his hands down and saw the blood running down his chest, now soaking his shirt. I wasn't sure if he had been stabbed in the heart, but I knew there was little time to lose.

"We have got to get you to the car. Now!" I said with as much urgency as I could make him understand.

I stood up and squatted down to wrap his right arm around my neck to help him stand up.

"I need you to stand up for me Jonah. I know it hurts," I yelled.

He struggled to get to one foot, and then the other, and the weight of his body pressed against me as I dragged him through the tall grass toward our car. I begged him to take just one more step and then another. The car felt like it was a mile away, but I knew I had to get him to the hospital at once. There was no time to lose.

The door opened to the little car, and I was able to get Jonah to sit down and I pushed his legs inside it. I ran to the driver's door and got in and started it up. I shifted the car into reverse and the car lurched backward and stalled. I looked over at Jonah, whose body had lunged forward.

"Sorry, babe. I don't really drive a stick shift," I told him.

"The...," he tried to say, pointing to the grassy area.

I ran to the grass and picked up the shovel and laid it in the backseat. I sat back down and looked toward Jonah. His breathing was very shallow and it was like his lungs had a leak. He would take one short, painful breath in, and let out a very long, controlled breath that took all of the energy he had to make that simple process that we take for granted work for him. I didn't know how long he could last.

"Jonah, are you still putting a lot of pressure against it?" I implored of him.

Jonah leaned forward and coughed, with blood shooting all over the dashboard. I had to get help now, and as we drove through this little town of Clare, I knew that the city of Cambridge might not be close enough. Jonah could bleed to death before we got there.

The dark drive seemed to go on forever, and Jonah continued to cough up blood. I had to do something fast. I could feel myself losing him. I pulled the car off to a side road and it jerked to a halt.

"Jonah, hang in there. I am going to fix this for you," I told him.

I got out of the car and grabbed the smaller scroll out of the trunk, and ran to Jonah's door. The blood had soaked his shirt and was continuing to run down his chest.

"Jonah, I need you to help me. I am going to get you out of the car. Can you help me do that? Just put your arm around me."

Jonah's feet were pulled out to the gravel road, and I summoned all of the strength that I could to pull him out of the car. He coughed again, and blood splattered all over my blouse.

We collapsed on the side of the road with gravel digging into our skin. Jonah fell on top of me with me landing on my back, and his back against my chest. I pushed my body up, taking him with me, so that he was leaning back against me. Jonah groaned a mighty groan.

"I need you to breathe slowly," I told him, and I wrapped my hand around his chest and pressed it against him, trying to slow the blood down.

I pulled the flashlight from my pocket and held it between my arm and ribcage, ensuring that my hands would be free. The small scroll was tucked inside my pocket and I pulled it out in front of both of us and aimed the flashlight toward it, and then I pulled the document from its housing.

"Jonah, I need you to repeat after me. I need you to say everything that I say to you. I know it hurts, baby. I know it is hard for you to breathe. But this is what we need to do. Can you do that for me?" I asked.

Jonah shook his head, not wanting to speak unless absolutely necessary. The blood was draining out of his body. My hands covered his wound, hoping that the pressure on it would be enough to slow down the flow. The light showing on the document was not steady at all, but that was all I could do.

And then I began to read.

Each word in the letter to King Abgar was spoken to Jonah, and then he would repeat it back to me in the best broken Greek that he could muster without the ability for him to even breathe.

Jonah slurred each word as he repeated them back to me. My heart knew that each second was a second closer to the end, but not the end that I had dreaded for the past week or more with him. He could die in my arms right here on the side of a road in England. I couldn't let that happen. The sound of bleating sheep could be heard close to us, and seemed to be getting closer, and I thought about watching him take pictures of those sheep on the side of the road along the beginning of our journey, how they seemed to be talking to him then, and now they had returned, only this time begging me to do everything in my power to make him live.

I flashed back to my time on church as a child and the exactness with which we memorized everything. I knew in my heart of hearts that that was what I needed Jonah to do at this moment. I needed perfection in him at the only moment since I had known him when he would be the most incapable of providing that. But I knew he tried. With each word, I could feel him struggle, not just Jonah trying to speak Greek, but the slurring of the words . I couldn't tell if he was saying everything right or not. I just had to continue with faith.

Jesus (in Greek then repeated), Jesus.

Of, of...

Nazareth, Nazareth.

It was over. We were finished, and I stopped and looked at my blood-soaked hands and wondered if I had done enough.

"Jonah, can you hear me?" I asked him, wanting to feel a nod of his head or something.

Suddenly, Jonah took a deep breath that filled his lungs, and coughed hard, but nothing came from his mouth. I turned my body to look at him from the side. I grabbed his face, and directed it toward me.

Jonah's eyes were barely open, and he coughed again.

"Where are we?" he asked.

"Are you kidding me?" I replied, "We are sitting on the side of the road somewhere between Clare and Cambridge."

"What? What happened?" he asked.

"What is the last thing that you remember, Jonah?"

"Um. We were getting ready to leave, and then Marco showed up. Is that right?" he asked.

"Yes, and then you jumped in front of me when Marco came toward me. He was going to stab me, and he stabbed you instead," I told him.

"Am I hurt? Am I bleeding?" he asked

"You were, and yes, you were a lot. Let me take a look at the wound," I said, pulling his shirt back exposing his upper chest.

"Where did it go?" I asked, moving my hand over the location of the gash. "You were stabbed right here." And I pointed to the area of Jonah's chest that I had felt with my own fingers, feeling the blood flowing down my own hand.

Now it was gone. There was a part of me that wanted so badly for this to be the outcome. That is why I pulled over and pulled Jonah from the car. But there was a part of me that would have never imagined that it could truly happen just like this. This experience that we had just had was something that was normally reserved for some crazy person you might hear on a radio show, or that of the legend of some people who lived in another time and another place.

But I then realized that healing can happen anywhere, during any time and at any place and in any season. I had witnessed it myself between Jonah and I; the healing process had begun and we had been the balm for each other's wounds.

With Jonah, his healing had begun with the touch of the tiniest seeds; the tiniest seed of faith.

Chapter 37

Elizabeth closed her eyes for the last time. Her breathing was shallow but her mind was still sharp. She lay on her back and her blankets were gathered up against her neck.

Her thoughts went to that night in Windsor Castle, and the first time she had seen the artifacts of Jesus Christ, mostly brought to England by Joseph of Arimathea, and her own grandfather King Edward I, bringing the Mandylion document back with him from his time in Jerusalem during The Crusades.

She remembered the stories of William the Conqueror, after his invasion, hearing that there were artifacts in England, and wanting to possess them. He hadn't found them, but this son had. She remembered the stories of the monarchy thinking the artifacts contained some secret power.

Her opportunity to possess them came when Elizabeth finally retired and had heard rumors that her uncle, King Edward II, needed money. Badly. All of the wars and his extravagant spending had bled the treasury dry, and Elizabeth had made her move.

She had offered to purchase everything that she had seen in that secret room at Windsor Castle from her uncle. Elizabeth had kept an ear on the comings and goings of the monarchy, knowing what they had and what they needed, and when she approached her uncle Edward had wanted more from Elizabeth, but money had become tighter and tighter. Finally, he gave in.

In the dark of night Elizabeth had gone alone and secured the artifacts, caring for them with the delicacy that they deserved, and stored them with a lock and key in a room next to her bedroom that no one else possessed a key to.

Then one day her thoughts went to what to do with everything once she was gone. Hiding them seemed to be the thing to do, hoping that someday someone would come along and could take over from where she left off.

Her tiny fingers grabbed the medallion that hung around her neck, clutching it tightly in her hands, and Elizabeth's lungs slowly released the last breath of air that was contained within them, slowly, until there wasn't anything left to breathe out and she passed away.

She had ordered the house nurse to not come into the room until the morning. In her mind, she had wanted to slip away in peace, and be alone with her thoughts, knowing that she had done everything in her life to keep sacred things sacred.

Chapter 38

I stood in the shower and watched the water run over my body. The water was dirty and dark red and then turned to a deep pink before finally changing to clear. If I hadn't had seen it with my own two eyes, I would have never believed it.

There was a four-inch cut in my shirt, and enough blood in my shirt and pants, not to mention the car, to donate to the Red Cross for a lifetime. I couldn't remember anything, but in my heart I knew what had happened. My heart had changed and I couldn't deny it.

I hadn't seen any of this coming. First the change of my heart toward Gabriela, and now this; I was just grateful and felt blessed that I was able to live through both experiences. I loved Gabriela, and I felt when I woke up that she was that woman. She was that woman that I wanted to be waking up in each time. She was the woman of my dreams.

I realized that I needed her in my life, however that was going to happen. We would cross that bridge when we needed to.

"Babe, there is something we need to do," I told Gabriela.

"What is that?" she asked.

"There is one more person that we need to see before this is over," I added.

I pickup up my cell phone and dialed the number.

"Hello. How are you?"

"You have?"

"How about tomorrow at noon?"

"Near the rose garden? Perfect. See you soon."

~

Our freshly cleaned MG pulled into the back parking lot of the Clare complex. Gabriela and I took the trunk out of the back of the car and carried it into the rose garden, and we sat.

"It feels like we have brought everything full circle, doesn't it to you?" Gabriela asked.

"Yes it does." I leaned toward her and kissed her lips.

A tall shadow grew close to us, and I looked up.

"Sister Victoria. How are you?" I asked.

"Fine. Very fine," she replied.

"Can we go inside? We have something for you," I said.

"Of course," was her response.

"Maude, do you have a room that we might be able to use?" Gabriela asked.

"Right this way, down the hall. First door on your right," she said while pointing her hand in the direction we should go.

The trunk was set down and we opened it up, showing Sister Victoria what we had discovered.

"This is a lock of the hair of Christ," Gabriela said, showing her the knotted strands. Sister Victoria's eyes became as wide as saucers.

"These are the sandals that he wore, and then here is his white robe," she continued.

"What are the scrolls?" Sister Victoria asked.

"The smaller of the two is a document that I think is referred to as the Mandylion document," I said while pulling it out.

I looked at it for the final time, seeing a faint bloody thumbprint on its edge, and as I looked closer I could see another print, but only in a faint darker black. Then I thought of King Abgar.

"You mean THE MANDYLION document?" she asked. "I never knew if it really existed."

"It exists," Gabriela added.

"This …," I said, and then stopped talking, and unrolled the painting of Jesus Christ.

Tears filled the eyes of Sister Victoria and she brought her hands to her mouth, covering her lips.

"I don't know what to say. This is miraculous! Thank you so much for showing them to me," she said with a hushed tone.

"We didn't bring you here to look at them," Gabriela answered.

"We brought you here to give them to you," I finished.

"Well...," she stammered for words. "I don't know what to say."

"You don't have to say anything," I said, placing everything back in the trunk.

"But don't you want something in return for them?" she asked.

"I got everything I have ever wanted," I said as I took Gabriela by the hand and looked at her and smiled.

"Thank you. Thank you both," she replied. "You will be greatly blessed."

"We already have been," Gabriela said, squeezing my hand.

In a bizarre story, Marco Balducci, known collector of ancient Roman antiquities, was found yesterday wandering the streets of Clare, England, blind and unable to speak. Authorities said that he had recently been released on bail with a pending charge of assault from an incident at a hotel in Glastonbury, but how or why he ended up in Clare is anyone's guess. Mr. Balducci is unable to speak, hear, or see, and authorities say that when he does try to eat he has trouble holding anything in his hands. Then after eating, he pulls at his tongue almost like it doesn't work anymore. Doctors say it is almost like he has lost all of the five basic senses. As more information is available on his condition, we will keep you informed. Christine Johnson, BBC News, London.

The airport was really busy, and Gabriela and I checked our bags and proceeded through security to our separate flights, hers heading to Naples, and mine to Boston.

"Jonah, I can't thank you enough for everything," she said.

"Gabriela, I wouldn't have wanted to be with anyone else," I replied. "Not ever."

And with that, she was gone. I watched her walk down the corridor until she disappeared in a crowd of people. We had made plans for her to come to Boston and visit during the holidays and see what might happen from there. But until then we would talk, Skype, and do whatever we had to to see what we could do to make this all work.

My trip to England had been one of apprehension as I arrived, and now I had a bitter taste of it as well as I prepared to leave. But it had been worth it, and I thought back to my empty apartment waiting for me when I got home, and how it was going to feel a lot more comfortable now. I had realized that you must first love yourself before you can feel the love from someone else. Gabriela had made me realize that, and that process had begun for me. I still had a long way to go, but I knew everything was going to work out perfectly.

I sat alone with my thoughts, and my email rang on my phone. It was a message from Mr. Throckmorton telling me that the painting Gabriela wanted from his antique store had been shipped to her home address. She would be surprised, and I couldn't wait to find out when it arrived.

My phone signaled that another message was in my inbox. It was an email from Lilly.

"Dad. Thank you so much for the Flat Lilly that you sent last night. I loved the picture. I loved the one with the painting of the man. It made me feel so good. You will have to tell me about him someday. I can't wait to see you. Love, Lilly."

In my mind, we had kept sacred things sacred, and I boarded the plane to Boston.

It was a cool fall day in central England, and Martin Locke was out walking his dog. It was the normal route for him, and the normal time of day. As he passed by the ruins of Castle Asbury, he stopped to rest for a few minutes. *No one is out today*, he thought. *It is getting too cold.*

He looked up at the old castle ruin, and for a split second something flashed in his eyes. It was a light, or more of a reflection. He walked closer to take another look. Underneath the second stair, normally hidden by the naked eye, was a rounded object that seemed to be out of place.

Martin ran his hands under the decaying stairs and felt something different. Without much work, it fell into his hand. He pulled it closer to his face. It was a medallion of sorts and he began to read:

T H A M E A I R A

Martin looked at his dog. "Chip, I have no idea what this is. But I think we might have something here."

THE END

About the Author

Kevin Hansen was born and raised in and around Boise, Idaho. He is the father of four amazing children, and spends his free time mountain biking, shooting pictures, and writing. An avid fan of the Los Angeles Dodgers, Kevin studied journalism with an emphasis on sports journalism.

He is currently working on his second book, roughly titled "My Last Will." Updates can be found on his Facebook pages The Healing Seed or Kevin Hansen Writer.

Questions and Answers with Kevin

Why did you write this book?

The Restoration of Jonah was originally born on the floor of my kitchen w. I love maps and had purchased a map book of England. I had copied the individual pages and was puzzle-piecing them together with clear packing tape to create a huge map. My mind began processing a few things and an idea materialized in my brain as the storyline for a movie. I had never written a screenplay before, so years later while in counseling, I was encouraged to write. So the novel experience began then.

Can you tell me about the book?

The Restoration of Jonah is a novel that is set in England about an American guy Jonah who teams up with an Italian girl Gabriela after stumbling upon what he believes to be a clue that could lead to a bigger treasure. If I may use this analogy, it is a Dan Brown kind of story written in a Nicholas Sparks writing style.

What did you learn while writing The Restoration of Jonah?

I learned a lot about myself and the issues that I had been dealing with in my life. As I would read back over the chapters I would see myself written through Jonah completely.

What was the writing process like for you?

It was an interesting experience. I typically write with pen and paper, and normally have classical music playing in my headphones while writing. I will make notations in the columns about the song(s) I was listening to while writing. I also don't outline chapters in advance. Everything comes to me and then right out the pen. I remember hearing a line once, "Write from your head, through your heart, then out your hand." I do that. I did paint myself into a couple corners, though, with certain clues in the story, then adding a second clue in the next chapter, then trying to figure out how they would go together.

Was the main character Jonah inspired by someone or something?

Jonah started out like any character in any other book, but as I would read back through chapters that I had finished, I saw myself in him a lot. Jonah is about 80-90 percent Kevin, and ultimately the kind of person that I think that I am, but also who I want to become.

What is next for Jonah and Gabriela?

That is a great question. I can see that there would be another book with them in it on another adventure, but I don't know yet. I think they are a perfect complement for the kind of work they did in the story.

What is next for you? Are you writing anything new?

I am writing two novels that dovetail into each other. They are nothing like The Restoration of Jonah, in that there are no historical references or influences in the story. They are more relationship stories with a concept that I really think the readers will love.

I am also putting together some ideas for a story that is completely historical fiction, set in 1800s Ireland.

43764206R00156

Made in the USA
Charleston, SC
04 July 2015